Brat Princess

KINGFISHER
a Houghton Mifflin Company imprint
222 Berkeley Street
Boston, Massachusetts 02116
www.houghtonmifflinbooks.com

First published in 2007
2 4 6 8 10 9 7 5 3 1

LIBRARY OF CONGRESS CATALOGING-IN-PUBLICATION DATA
has been applied for.

ISBN: 978-0-7534-6132-7

Printed in India
1TR/0707/THOM/SCHOY/60BNWP/C

Zodiac Girls

Brat Princess

Cathy Hopkins

KINGFISHER
BOSTON

Chapter One
Welcome to my world

"No. I am not ready. Do I look like I'm ready?"

I was lying on a sun lounger by the pool at our villa in St. Kitts in the Caribbean, my cell phone in one hand, a chocolate milk shake in the other. Coco was lying on the lounger next to mine, also wearing sunglasses. She's my dog—a pink bichon frisé. (Everyone at my last school had a little dog, but no one had theirs dyed the way I had. I had to do something—all the pooches looked the same, white and cute—but now Coco stands out in a crowd and matches my new nail color *perfectly*.)

I'd just been thinking how utterly cool life was here on this paradise island, when I was suddenly interrupted by a question as to whether I was ready to leave. Anyone with half a brain should have been able to see that I was in no way prepared to board a flight to Europe. Like, what kind of idiot would travel to Paris in a turquoise bikini, even if it is from Prada's new collection and on everyone's must-have list for the season? We used to live in England when I was younger, so I know how cold it can get in that part of the world. Like, Brrrfreezingville.

"Sorry, Miss Hedley-Dent, but . . ." whined Henry. (He's my dad's chauffeur, personal assistant, and handyman, though you'd hardly know it. In his usual garb of Bermuda shorts and Hawaiian shirt and with his shoulder-length blond hair, he looks more like a professional surfer than a servant.)

"What now, Henry?" I was beginning to get annoyed and would have been more snappy if it wasn't for the fact that my friend Tigsy was on hold, waiting for me, on the other end of the phone.

"Just, um . . . the plane has been ready for some time, and the pilot has been waiting for you for more than an hour."

"So? Tell him that he may have to wait another hour because I'm not ready, and I want to catch some more rays before I leave."

"May I at least give him some idea of when you may be ready for takeoff?"

I gave Henry my best withering look. Tigs and I'd practiced it for ages in the mirror at school last year before I got expelled. One eyebrow up, nostrils breathing in, and lips tight. Tigsy said that I appeared more constipated than angry when I did the "look," but, whatever, Henry got the message, backed out of the room, and closed the door. He's so pathetic when he does that droning-on thing. Like, schedules . . . airports . . . Like, it's my problem. Not.

At last I could resume my call. I lay back on the lounger, took a sip of my milk shake, and *yuck* . . . I spat it out. It was WARM!

"Shirla. SHIRLA!" I called.

A few minutes later, Shirla, our Caribbean housekeeper, came out of the house. She always does everything sooo slowly. Like it's all one mighty effort. Probably owing to the fact that she weighs around five million pounds. She's like a house on legs. Legs that are made of jelly—she doesn't so much walk as wobble her way along. I pointed at the glass. "More ice. And a dab more chocolate."

"Ooh, you likes the chocolate. If you not careful, girl, you going to become one big melted chocolate in that sun," she said as she swayed over, took the glass, and then sashayed off toward the kitchen.

"Oh, and can you get Mason to make me some fries before the flight takes off? Those big square ones he does. And bring a little pot of that yummy sour-cream-and-chive dip to dunk them in. And something for Coco." (Mason's our cook and Shirla's husband. They're an odd couple; he's as skinny as she is large.)

Shirla stopped for a moment. "Uh, I guess I could," she said, "but you ought to eat some greens one of these days, or else them pimples on your chin there are going to be breaking out all over your pretty little face. And don't you go giving that dog no chocolate neither. It ain't right." She tutted to herself and then disappeared inside before I could say anything.

I picked up the phone again.

"Yum. Fries," said Tigsy on the other end. "Think I'll get our maid to make me some. I love fries."

"Sorry, Tigs, guess you heard all that? Like, welcome to my world. Can you believe it? Henry trying to tell *me* when we have to leave—like, who pays who around here?"

"*Exactement*," said Tigsy. "You have to let them know who's boss, yeah?"

"Yeah. It's Mommy's fault. She's way too nice with them all. Like a little mouse. She's like, um, pardon me for squeaking. And Dad's never here, so what can we expect? It's left to me to let them know who's in charge, like I haven't got enough to do as it is."

"Totally."

I stared out over the infinity pool and the ocean beyond. It was glistening with a thousand tiny stars in the afternoon sun. "Yeah. Like, sometimes I think that just because I'm only fourteen, they, like, think they can tell me what to do. But I say, no way. No way."

"Yeah. No way. Um, but, Leonora, I'm not being difficult or anything, but one thing I do know is that sometimes when you're traveling, like, having a tantrum can work against you. Like, it's the beginning of December, coming up to Christmas, right?"

"Yeah. Like, deck the halls with boughs of holly, blah-de-blah-de-blah, de-blah-de, yawn."

"So everyone's on the move, yeah? Not just us?"

"I guess."

"Well, I know from when Daddy does his own bookings for when we land our little jet that, if you miss your slot, especially at busy times, you don't get another one."

"Oh. *Un problema*, you think? So you're saying what exactly?"

Tigsy laughed on the other end of the phone. "That you'd better get your filthy rich butt off that island in the Caribbean, Leonora Hedley-Dent, and onto the jet, or else we're not going to be able to do our shopping trip in Paris and get back in time for Christmas."

"Like I care about Christmas. Bah humbug to all that, I say. It's just *another* excuse for the staff to skip work for the day," I said, but I did get up, slip my feet into my Gucci mules with the kitten heels, and make my way through the open French doors to my bedroom. Coco got up and followed me. She's sooooo cute. She walks like she's wearing heels too.

"I know," said Tigsy. "Three weeks to go, and it will all be one big bore, as usual. The fun part will be you being here and the shopping beforehand, although there will be presents on the day. Daddy said that he might get me a new diamond Cartier watch this year. I've put it on my list since I am getting tired of my Rolex. It's so last season. But really, Lee Lee, I mean, I'm going to be okay for getting to Paris. I'm in Geneva and only have to hop on a train to get there."

"It's cool. I get you. I'll get a move on," I said as I took a couple of candy bars out of a drawer and flung them into a suitcase on the bed. "I'm packing as we speak, but I'm not going to let Henry think that I'm doing it for him."

"No. 'Course not. But please hurry. I've got no one to play with over here."

"I'll see you tomorrow."

"Excellent. Kissy, kissy. Daddy's booked us the whole top floor at the George the Fifth Hotel. I've been there before, when Imelda Parker Knowles had her sixteenth birthday party there during the summer. It's way cool. I think you'll like it."

"Sorreee. Packing. Be there. Bysie-bye."

"Bysie-bye."

I put my phone down by the bed and went to the mirror, spritzed on some of my Goddess perfume, picked up my brush, and brushed through my hair. I was pleased with the way it was looking. The sun had made my new blond highlights even lighter. One day Shirla had seen me before I'd used my hair straighteners. She said that I had fabulous hair. Ha! She has no idea about the work it takes to keep it looking good. Like, I would be mortified if anyone saw me with my hair in its natural state (curly-wurly), but she said that it suited my birth sign, which is Leo—and my hair, which is halfway down my back, is like a tawny lion's mane. *Huh. Like, why exactly would I want to look like a lion, for heaven's sake?* I thought as I applied a slick of mascara. *Most of them have mangy manes, hardly the honey-and-fudge organic highlights that Daniel Blake, stylist to the stars, runs through mine!*

I put in my blue-tinted contact lenses to cover my boring brown eyes, applied some concealer over my zits, and glanced around to see what else needed to be done. Coco was watching my every move.

"Oh, don't look at me like that, boo-boo," I said. "I'll only be gone a few days."

Coco rolled over on her back and wiggled on the bed. She's so sweet, even if her belly is a different color from the rest of her. (I ran out of dye.)

Mommy and Shirla had done most of my packing, but I threw in a few more things, just in case. All essentials that they'd missed. Lip-gloss. Latest chill-out CD. More candy bars for emergencies. I glanced over at the photo in the silver frame by my bed. *Can't forget to pack that*, I thought. I never went anywhere without it. It was of me and Poppy, my sister. It was taken when I was 12 and she was ten. Oh. Hair straighteners. I threw them in on top. I couldn't believe that they'd forgotten them, although, actually, I could—another example of how nobody around here has a clue about what matters to me. To travel without them would be like losing an arm or a leg; they're that important. It was hard to know what else I'd need, though. Tigsy said it was unseasonably warm in Europe, but it wouldn't be as hot as it was here in St. Kitts. The only clothes that I'd worn for the past week were bikinis and sarongs. Still. If it got too cold, I could buy some new cashmere sweaters. I'd worn the ones I got last December at least three times during the winter season, so I was due for a few new ones.

I pulled my fave pair of skinny jeans out of the closet and began to put them on. Erg. Arff. They were supposed to be tight, but not that tight!

"MOMMY!!!!"

Mommy appeared at the door a few seconds later. "Yes, darling?"

"My jeans! They've shrunk."

Mommy came in and watched me struggling to get the jeans zipped up.

"Um . . . you don't think, darling, that you could have maybe put on a teeny-weeny bit of weight, do you?"

I could feel a tantrum coming on. I could feel it in the pit of my stomach, bubbling and boiling like a volcano about to erupt—like, it was all right for her; she never put on an ounce of fat, no matter what she ate. She was so lucky, with her straight blond hair and her perfect figure. She didn't look her age either, and people always thought that we were sisters. As if. It soooo wasn't fair that I'd inherited Dad's frumpy genes and his stupid curly hair instead of hers. "Me? Put on weight? These are MY BEST JEANS. I HAD TO WAIT THREE MONTHS ON A LIST FOR THEM TO COME IN TO THE STORE, AND THAT STUPID HOUSEKEEPER HAS SHRUNK THEM IN THE WASH!"

For a split second, I swear that I saw a hint of a smile cross Mommy's face, which made me even madder. She put her hand on my arm. "Now calm down," she said in a soft voice that made me want to hit something. "You're a growing girl . . ."

I brushed away her hand. "Calm DOWN? Growing GIRL? I CAN'T GROW ANY MORE. I'M *ENORMOUS* AS IT IS."

Mommy sighed. "You've got a lovely figure, Leonora, and fabulous long legs. You're . . ."

"WHAT DO YOU KNOW? I'M ALREADY A SIZE SIX, AND EVERYONE IN MY CLASS IS A FOUR OR A TWO! And Lottie James is even a size ZERO! I'M AN ELEPHANT! MY WHOLE DAY IS RUINED. I HATE YOU. YOU NEVER UNDERSTAND."

I wiggled out of the jeans. They wouldn't zip up no matter how much I yanked at the zipper. I tossed them onto the bed and then threw myself, face-down, on after them. And then I went for it.

"WaaaaaaARRRRGGHHHHHHHHHHHHHH HHHHHHHHHHHHHHH."

I thrashed my arms, pummeled my pillows, and threw my legs up and down. And then I felt sick. Yes, I was going to throw up. I could feel it. I sat up. "And now I FEEL SICK."

Mommy looked at me with wide eyes and an expression of terror. *Why, oh, why can't she ever say or do the right thing when I feel like this?* I wondered. *I'm sure I'm adopted. I can't be her daughter. We're nothing like each other, and she doesn't have a clue what to do with me.* My head started to throb. "And now I've got a headache," I wailed. "And I'm fat. And have zits. And it's all your FAULT!"

At that moment, there was a gentle knock on the door, and Henry poked his head around. I picked up a pillow and threw it at him.

"GET OUT! GET OUT. ALL OF YOU. OUT. *OUT.* I HATE YOU ALL."

Henry disappeared mega fast, and Mommy scurried out like a frightened rabbit.

"WahurggghhhhhhhhhHHHH!" I yelled at the ceiling. "*No one* understands me. Not *anyone.* I *hate* everyone. I hate them all. I hate my life. I'm so ugly. And *fat.* I am soooooooooooooo unhappy."

14

Chapter Two
Rules for life

Rule one: I am going to go on a diet. A serious diet. In fact, I'm not going to eat anything until I am a size zero like Lottie. Or . . . hmm . . . Maybe there's some miracle fat-diluting pill that Mommy could get me. Yes, there must be. Or maybe liposuction? Cassidy Poole at my last school had her butt done over Easter break. She couldn't sit down for weeks when she came back after the vacation. So maybe not that option. I so don't do pain.

Rule two: No member of staff must look at me until I am a size zero.

Rule three: Shirla must not use that perfume that she wears. It smells like vanilla and cocoa, and that makes me want to EAT chocolate.

Rule four: Shirla must come with me to Europe, since she is the only person I can stand to have around me at the moment (as long as she doesn't wear that perfume!).

I was ready for my trip, sitting on the patio with Coco and waiting for the car to take me to the plane. I was using the time to come up with some rules to make my life more bearable. Not that anyone cared, aside from Coco, who adores me. They were all too busy with their own lives. Daddy hadn't even called this morning to say goodbye. Too busy making millions. Still, I suppose someone has to. He works with banks, and although he'd tried a few times to explain what he does, I still don't get it. It has something to do with markets and shares and money going up and down. Whatever. Who cares? We're loaded. That's what counts. I have my own savings account with hundreds of thousands of dollars in it.

Mommy had been busy with Shirla in the kitchen, figuring out the menus for Christmas Day. She was having a bunch of boring neighbors over this year and came out onto the patio laden down with cookbooks. I so wasn't interested—like, Christmas in the Caribbean? It's not right. There should be snow, but even in Europe it hadn't snowed at Christmastime for years and years.

"All ready, honey?"

I nodded curtly. I hadn't forgotten how unsympathetic she'd been about my weight gain, and, come to think of it, she hadn't asked me what *I* wanted for Christmas dinner like she usually did. Not that it mattered anymore, because I'd be having a lettuce leaf and hot water with a slice of lemon. That was all that Madison Peters had for a whole term at my last school, and she was as thin as a rail. Miserable, she was, but, then, I would be too if that's all I had for weeks at a time. I was quickly going off my diet idea. Thinking about my last school made me feel sad for a moment. It was the fifth school that I had been expelled from in just over two years, and it was where I had met Tigsy. I would be sad to have to start another school without her—that is, if Mommy and Daddy can find me somewhere that hasn't blacklisted me. Whatever. I guess I can always try homeschooling. Lots of people do it, although I've heard it said that homeschoolers can sometimes lack social skills on account of not having mixed with other people. I wouldn't want that to happen to me. The last thing I'd want is to be thought of as lacking social skills or being difficult. I can be firm and strong-minded but never difficult. Not me.

"And thanks for asking what *I* want for Christmas dinner," I said to Mom.

"Oh, didn't I? Oh. I meant to. Are you sure I didn't? Hmm. Oh . . ." Mommy blustered on, obviously embarrassed by the fact that she'd forgotten to ask me. I decided to put her out of her misery.

"Well, actually, you don't need to include me in *any* of the Christmas meals, since I won't be having any."

17

She looked shocked. "What do you mean, Leonora?"

"Diet. I am on one from now on. I won't be eating again for at least a month."

Shirla came out behind her and overheard me. She was carrying my plate of delicious-looking fries. "Ah. So you won't be wanting these, then?" She dipped a big juicy one in the dip and popped it into her mouth. I felt my mouth water as I watched her lick her lips. I *love* eating. It is one of my few pleasures in life. So sad that I will have to suffer and deny myself just so that I can look good in my jeans. Never was there a truer sentence than: You have to suffer to be beautiful. But . . . maybe I could start tomorrow. No. That would be difficult being in Paris and in a hotel. Shame to miss out. Best time to start it completely is when I get back. Or in the new year. Yeah. That's always a good time to start with diets. Resolutions and all that.

"Um . . . Well. Maybe I should just force something down before I go," I said. "And Mason did go to all that trouble of making them, Shirla." (Never let it be said that I don't appreciate what people do for me. I do.)

Shirla turned to go back inside. "No problem, dahlin'. Me likes the fries too. Um, uh, they's good."

I made myself take a deep breath. "Shirla, give

me that plate RIGHT now," I commanded. "And you'd better go and pack a suitcase. I've decided that I want you to come with me to Europe."

Shirla stopped and looked questioningly at Mommy.

"But Henry is going with you. It's all been arranged," said Mommy.

"I don't care," I said. "I want Shirla. It's only for two days."

Shirla shook her head. "I's not going to Europe. Oh, no, sugar. I's got things to do, Mrs. Hedley-Dent. My little Mariah. She in the nativity play tomorrow night. She being a camel. I can't miss that, not for all the pea in China."

"Tea, Shirla," I said. "It's *tea* in China, and, anyway, there wasn't a camel in the nativity. There was a donkey, though."

Shirla laughed. "Her costume got four legs, that's all I know. And she sure look like a camel, and I ain't missing her, not for you, not for nobody. It's bad enough she didn't get the part she wanted, which was the Christmas angel, so I ain't missing it. No, siree."

Typical, I thought. *As usual, everyone is thinking about themselves.*

Mommy had on her frightened-rabbit look. "Yes, it's all been arranged," she said.

At that moment, there was a sound at the front of the villa, and Mommy ran out to see who it was.

I turned to Shirla. "You *will* come with me," I said. "I can *make* you."

Shirla laughed, raised an eyebrow, did a perfect withering look, and shook a finger at me. "Just you try, sugar. Just you try. This is ma' granddaughter's first nativity play. I ain't missing that."

"Well *that* is your problem, Shirla. Don't make it mine. And by the way . . . I lent you one hundred dollars last week. I'm sure Mommy wouldn't like it if she knew about that! The staff borrowing money?"

"I ain't forgotten," said Shirla. She reached into the pocket of her apron and produced ten ten-dollar bills.

"Um . . . I don't think so. I want interest on it," I said. We did a class on economics at my last school. I knew all about lending and borrowing money. Our teacher had said that only a fool didn't ask for interest.

For a moment, Shirla looked as if she wanted to throw the plate at me, but she held back and put her money back in her pocket. "Okay, missy. So how much interest you want, then?"

"Five percent."

Shirla shook her head and tutted and then she

handed the fries to me. "Uh-uh," she said as she turned and wobbled toward the kitchen. "Oo-ee. You sure is one precious madam. Uh-uh, you is."

"And where's my princess?" boomed a voice from the front of the villa.

Seconds later, Daddy appeared. I didn't even bother to look up, although I could see from out of the corner of my eye that he had on his work suit, so he must have come from his office.

"What are you doing here?" I asked.

"Come to see my girl off," he said.

"But I'll be back in a couple of days," I said. "You've never come home to see me off before."

Mommy shot Daddy a "look," as if they'd been caught. *They're up to something*, I thought. *Probably getting me some secret Christmas present. Hope it's not another horse. If it is, I hope they get the right color this time*. They got me a white one for my birthday, and he had to go back because Mercedes Bernshaw had a white one, and no way was I going to be accused of copying that loser.

"Come on, give your dad a hug," said Daddy, holding out his arms.

I could hear that the car had arrived at *last*, so I got up and pushed past him. "Get real. I'm too old for hugs now," I said as he lost his balance and toppled over into a flower bed.

An hour later I was on the plane and on my way. *What a relief*, I thought, inhaling the comfortingly expensive scent of the leather upholstery as we took off into the sky. Mommy and Daddy had been acting really weird, like they'd taken lovey-dovey pills or something. Mommy was all clingy, more so than usual, like, "Oh, my darling girl," and stroking my hair. Like, *ew!* I so don't do emotional. (Except with Coco. I was sad to leave her.) It was especially embarrassing with Mommy and Daddy because there was a tall, handsome, suntanned man with a mane of dark hair at the hangar who was watching me, as if he couldn't take his eyes off me. Okay, so he was way too old for boyfriend material—like, maybe old enough to be my dad, even— but he had the X factor and probably recognized a kindred spirit in me, since I also have it. I think that he was a celebrity. He looked familiar—possibly an actor on TV. It would have been something to brag about when I went back to school, that is, if I'd had a school to be going back to. Or a bunch of friends to brag to, in fact. I did, once upon a time, but that was a long time ago. My sister Poppy and I had tons of friends, and our house always used to be full of people, but I wasn't going to let myself think about then. It never did any good. I blinked back sudden tears and steeled myself. Past is past. Gone.

As the plane burst through the clouds, though,

I couldn't help but wonder what had come over Daddy. He was usually like me. Mr. Unemotional. But even *he* had given me a big hug (when he had climbed out of the flower bed), as if he was going to miss me for once. Maybe they were both worried that the plane might crash or something. Whatever. I hadn't responded to either of their overly clingy goodbyes—like, why should I pretend that I was going to miss them? They didn't really care about me. If they did, they would have forced Shirla to come with me. A small request, that's all I had made. I liked Shirla. She's so totally a nonpushover type of person, and I had to respect that, although I didn't let her know that. *But no point moping over it*, I decided as I put all thoughts of St. Kitts out of my head. I looked out the window. Despite the bad start the day had gotten off to, I couldn't help feeling excited. Tigsy was a lot of fun. Okay, so she wasn't Poppy, but we were going to have a great time in Paris.

To pass the flight time, I added up my accounts and figured out who owed me what.

Shirla: $100
Henry: $250
Mason: $200

Plus interest at five percent. I figured it out on my little calculator. It's a tiny pink one. Designer, of course. So cute. Cost a fortune. To get five percent, you multiply by .05. Cool. And if they don't pay me back by January, I will put the interest up another percent. *Mommy and Daddy would be so pleased that my education wasn't totally wasted*, I thought as I tucked away my notebook.

There were still hours to go, so I read a few magazines, watched a DVD, snoozed a little, and ate a few of the assorted canapés that had been prepared by Mason before we left. I had to send a couple of things back—like, when will they get that I don't eat avocados? I so don't do slime. I've told Henry again and again. As a punishment for him accompanying me instead of Shirla, I made him give me a manicure. When he'd finished, I told him that I hated the color and redid my nails myself. After that, I watched another movie and then dozed off again and woke to feel my ears pop. *Ah. We must be starting to land*, I thought, as I took a peek outside the window. I'd been to Paris before, and one of my favorite parts was seeing it come into view from the plane.

"Fasten your seat belts, as we will be landing shortly," came Pete the pilot's voice over the intercom.

We were still above the clouds, so there was nothing to see as the plane continued its descent, but I kept looking, and at last we burst through the clouds, and I could see the ground below. *What?*

Fields and fields of green. What's going on here? Where's the Eiffel Tower? We must be coming in at a different angle from my previous trips, I thought, as I felt the wheels beneath the plane come out, ready for landing. *I never realized that Paris had so much countryside around it.*

"Plane ready for landing. Staff, take your seats," came Pete's voice.

Henry came in from the kitchen area, took his seat on the opposite side of the compartment, and strapped himself in. I continued looking out the window. "Hey, Henry. Have we been diverted to another airport outside Paris?"

Henry looked down at the floor.

"Henry?"

He looked as if he was having a nervous attack with his eyes and didn't know where to look. His eyes rotated around from his shoes to the overhead racks to the window. Up, down, around, but he wouldn't meet my eyes.

"Well?" I asked again.

"Um. Yes. Slight diversion, I think. Slight. Yes . . ."

"You *think*? But why? Why didn't anyone tell me?"

"Sleeping," squeaked Henry. "You were sleeping."

"Don't worry, Henry. I'm not going to be angry, I just like to be kept informed. Is there bad weather? Fog? What is it? Snow?"

Henry was looking really peculiar. "Um. No.

Temperatures are cold, but no, no snow."

Maybe he's a bad flier, I thought, *but . . . we've flown together before, and he's never acted like this.* "Are you okay, Henry?"

"Oh, yes," said Henry, looking anything but okay.

I looked out the window again and got a strange feeling that we weren't over France at all. The fields below looked remarkably like . . . like England! I knew it well, since three of my schools had been there. A feeling of panic hit my stomach. *There's something going on that Henry isn't telling me about. Oh, God, the plane is going down. Must be engine trouble. Why else would we be landing here? Oh, God, that's why Henry looks freaked out. He knows. Are we going to make it? Oh, God. I'm too young to die.*

I gripped the sides of my seat. "Tell me, Henry, tell me the truth. We're going to crash, aren't we? How bad is it?"

Henry kept staring ahead. He still wouldn't even look at me. *Must be really bad,* I thought.

"HENRY. *ANSWER ME.*"

I was beginning to feel really scared by now and felt a tantrum coming on. I hit the pause button on it. *Not the time,* I thought, as I looked out the window again. We were coming in to land at a small airport. Definitely not Charles de Gaulle. *Ah, non, certainement non.* I had been there, and this wasn't it. Not by a million miles. This looked more like a private airport. *Where are we?*

As the plane landed with a soft bump on the runway, the brakes screamed on, slowing us down, and then we began to cruise toward a hangar and a small building. *Not crashed, then*, I thought. *Or maybe just one engine was in trouble, and we had to make an early landing, and Henry didn't want to scare me. That's okay.* I made myself take a deep breath.

"I'm okay, Henry. Now, all I need to know is what is going on. That's not too much to ask now, is it?"

Henry shook his head, unclasped his seat belt, stood up, and began to walk past me. "Sorry," he mouthed as he disappeared out of the cabin.

Sorry? Sorry? What for? My mind went into overdrive. I quickly pulled out my phone and turned it on, ready to call Tigsy and then Mommy. Before I could punch in Tigsy's number, the cabin door opened, and the celebrity man who had been staring at me back in St. Kitts was standing there. *How did he get onboard?* I wondered as he beamed a bright smile, revealing a set of Hollywood teeth. Then it dawned on me. *Ah! Hijacked. That's what's happened, and Henry's in on it. I never trusted him. Probably in it for the money. Happens all the time. He's always borrowing money, and he can never pay it back. Oh, God, how completely pathetic.*

"You won't be needing that where you're going,

27

miss," said the strange man as he strode over to me, reached down, and took my phone. "Now, if you'd like to get up and come with me."

Chapter Three

Pas Paris

"Who are you?"

Silence.

"Where are you taking me?"

Silence.

We were whizzed through customs, and I found myself in the back of a car. A car with tinted windows so that I could see out but no one could see in. Celebrity man was in the front, and between us was a glass partition, but I could see that there was a gap in it through which he could hear me. There was no doubt about it—I had been kidnapped. I had done my best to resist getting off the plane, but the man had simply picked me up, put me over his shoulder, and carried me out to the car as if I was as light as a feather. Of course, I kicked and thumped, but it seemed to have no effect at all. The man was a monster. Or wearing body armor. Whichever, his broad shoulders didn't seem to feel my protests.

"Can I have my phone back?"

Silence.

"I need to use the bathroom."

Silence.

"Look, my parents are very rich, but you probably know that already. They will pay you off, no doubt about it. I even have my own account with thousands in it, so how about we don't waste any more time, you let me speak to them, we'll get your money sorted out, and I can be on my way to Paris to meet my friend?"

More silence.

"Where's Henry? I suppose he put you up to this?"

Still no reply. I felt a tantrum coming on. "WeeeraaaarrrgHHHHHHHHHHHHHHHHHHHH HHHHHHHHHHHH!" I blasted out. I pummeled the seats. Kicked the back of the front seats. Thrashed around. The man didn't even notice. Not one bit. He didn't even turn around. *Hmm. Tantrum tactic not working,* I thought. *Best save my energy for later.*

I leaned forward to tap on the glass partition. And that was when I saw that he was listening to an iPod. No *wonder* he wasn't responding.

"Hey, dingbat brain!" I yelled, but he was warbling along to some tune, totally oblivious to me in the back. I knocked on the partition again. Nothing.

I had no choice but to sit back and look out the window. It was beginning to get dark outside, but I could see that the area was rural. We drove through a village with stores, and the houses looked warm and cozy as people turned on lights, and through one window, I glimpsed a family gathering around a fire. I saw a sign for the village as we left it behind. Osbury? *Osbury—sounds vaguely familiar*, I thought and made a mental note of it so that I could tell my rescuers later. After the village, the road got dark again, and we made our way through hedges and narrow roads. *We are totally out in the country*, I thought, as we sped along. *I wonder where X-factor man is taking me.*

After another 15 minutes there was some movement in the front. I leaned forward to see that the driver had taken off his headphones.

"Hey," I said.

"Hey," he replied.

"Did you hear any of what I was saying before?"

"A little. Who? Why? Where? Yeah. Heard all that. That's why I put on my headphones. Henry's on his way back to St. Kitts. He had nothing to do with this."

"So who are you?"

"Name's Sonny Olympus."

I burst out laughing. "Sonny Olympus! What kind of stupid name is that?"

Sonny looked upset. "My name!" he replied, and then he pouted like a spoiled, sulky teenager. "And it is so *not* stupid. If you've really got a problem, though, you can call me Mr. O., but only if you *have to.*"

I laughed again. My tactic was to make him feel

inferior. It works on most people. "*Mr. O.!* Pff. Also a stupid name. So who are you, anyway?"

He turned and said proudly. "I am, or will be, like a ray of sunshine in your life. I am to be your guardian for a month."

"Oh, get a life," I said. "I'm a bit old for guardians, wouldn't you say?" But something he said had panicked me. A month. Whoever was behind this, Mr. O. or a whole bunch of them, they planned to keep me for a *month*. No way. Outside, the scenery looked bleak, like we were driving through the moors. I felt a trickle of fear, and, as a hundred horror stories began to play through my mind, I tried not to imagine what could happen to me in such a remote place.

"You did hear that my parents are very rich . . . ?" I began.

"Yep, heard that part. And you've got thousands. Lucky old you."

"So as soon as you call Mommy and Daddy, they'll pay."

For some reason, Mr. O. seemed to think that I had said something hysterical and guffawed loudly.

"WHY are you laughing?"

"Oh, I think you'll find that they've paid already," he said in a really spiteful way. *Just who is this guy?* I wondered.

"*Paid already?* What do you mean?"

"Room and board. Hey, relax, kid. You'll see soon enough."

"Don't call me 'kid.' And *relax*? Are you from another planet?"

This caused Mr. O. to laugh more than ever. "Yes. Yes, indeed I am," he said. "How *observant* of you."

Rude, sulky, and sarcastic, and all in under an hour, I thought. *Boy! This guy could almost outdo me!*

He was starting to *really* annoy me. *Time to try another tactic,* I decided. I leaned forward and caught his eye in the driver's mirror. He smiled. I smiled back. "You really are very handsome, you know . . ." I began. Flattery usually gets you everywhere, and all I needed was to get him wrapped around my little finger.

Mr. O. nodded his head. "Yes, I do know. People tell me all the time."

Modest, too. Not. "I'm sure they do," I said. "Now, Mr. O., if you are nice to me, I'll be nice to you, and . . ."

"Oh, for heaven's sake, cut it out. You're too old to be playing such a childish game."

"Fine, so how old are you, then?"

Mr. O. snorted. "Couple of thousand centuries. You?"

"Fourteen."

"Exactly. I rest my case."

"Anyway, that's stupid. You can't be a couple of thousand centuries old. That's not possible."

"There are more things in heaven and earth than are

dreamt of in your philosophy, kid," said Mr. O.

"Oh, yeah? Says who? And *don't* call me 'kid'."

"Pal of mine by the name of William Shakespeare."

Oh, good grief, I thought. *He thinks that he's centuries old and a friend of Shakespeare's. He's crazy.*

"I have my own money, you know, Mr. O. . . ." I began again.

"I know. You said. Lesson number one. Money can't buy you everything, and you'd better believe me, it won't where we're going," he said as we rounded a corner, and I glimpsed the lights of a building ahead. It was hard to see in the dark, but it looked like an old fortress on top of a hill. The lights were on and cast a warm glow out into the dark night. *Our hotel,* I thought as Mr. O. drove up and stopped the car. *At least it looks like they're going to hide me somewhere decent.*

"I can walk," I said when Mr. O. opened the back of the car. "Just get my bags, will you?"

Mr. O. laughed and mimicked me, saying, *"Get my bags, will you?"* in a whiny voice as he held the door open for me. He indicated the porch at the front of the lodge, as if to say that I should go in there. I took a quick look around to see if I could escape. The pale crescent moon behind the silhouettes of trees didn't give off much light, but I could just about see gardens all around, although the shrubs were dense black. I decided that I'd have a better look in the morning and make a run for it when I had a better idea of where I was.

Mr. O. followed me up to the porch, *without* bringing in my bag, I noticed. The door was opened by a tall, black, athletic-looking man with a shaved head and a chiseled jaw line. In the combat gear he was wearing, he had the appearance of a soldier, and, like Mr. O., he was incredibly handsome. Buff, as Tigsy would say.

As soon as we got inside the wood-paneled reception area and the man had closed the door, I ran over and hid behind him. I didn't like where I was. The whole building looked shabby and smelled of mold and mushrooms. On a battered table in a corner was a potted plant with half of its leaves dried up due to lack of care. This wasn't a place I wanted to stay in for a moment longer than was necessary.

"Quick, get the police," I said, as I pointed at Mr. O. "That man has kidnapped me."

"Is that right?" the man in combat gear said, chuckling. I nodded.

Mr. O. rolled his eyes as if he was exasperated, and then he examined his nails as if he was bored with me. "Now, why would you think that?" he asked.

"Duh? I'm in a strange country, brought here in a strange car by a *stranger*. You do the math."

"You haven't been kidnapped, Leonora," said the new man.

"How do you know my name? Oh, *no*. You're in on it too. Who are you, then?"

"My name is Mario. I will be running the program."

"*Program?!* What program?"

Mario turned to Mr. O. "You haven't told her yet?"

Mr. O. shook his head.

"No. He hasn't told me anything. What kind of hotel is this, exactly?"

Mario laughed. "Hotel? *Hotel?*" He held up his arms to indicate our surroundings. "This isn't a hotel. At least, not any longer. Oh, no. Those days are long gone. Now it's a boot camp."

"A *boot camp?*"

Mr. O. and Mario nodded.

I felt an awful sinking feeling in my stomach. "And why am I here, exactly?" I asked, although I was beginning to get the picture.

And it wasn't looking good.

Chapter Four

Queen of Sheba

"Look, let's get this sorted out, and then we can all be on our way. Let me speak to my mother. Um. Please."

Mario and Mr. O. exchanged looks.

"You told her the real news yet?" asked Mario.

Mr. O. shook his head.

"*Real* news? What are you talking about?"

"Later," said Mr. O. "All in good time."

"Two calls," said Mario and handed me a portable phone from a hatch in the wall, through which I glimpsed a drab-looking office, full of files and cardboard boxcs.

I took the phone and walked over to the corner. I had a bad feeling about what was happening and was totally unsure about how to play it. These guys might be über good-looking, but they also looked as if they meant business. And they might think that calling it "boot camp" was some kind of funny joke, but I knew what was going on. I'd been kidnapped. I needed Mommy to get me out, and fast. I dialed her number, and she picked up right away, as if she'd been standing by the phone.

"Is that you, Leon–?"

"Mommy, thank God. Shut up and listen. You have to act quickly because I don't know how long I have, but I've been kidnapped. I'm not sure where they've brought me, but I'm pretty sure that it's England somewhere, since all of the road signs and billboards are in English. I'm close to a village called Osbury. Wasn't that close to where we used to live when I was little? It looked familiar. Anyway, check it out and trace this call. Get the police on it, and get them on it *fast*. I don't like it here. It's spooky, and I don't know what these men have planned. There are two of them so far, but there may be others."

There was silence on the other end of the phone.

"Mommy?"

"Yes. Yes, darling, I'm here . . ." She sounded as if she'd been crying. *So the dirty rotten scoundrels have been in touch already*, I thought. *Probably demanding their ransom.* Still. I didn't know why she was crying. We could surely afford it, whatever it was.

There was a commotion on the other end, and Daddy came on.

"Leonora?"

"Yes, Daddy. Did you hear? I've been kidnapped. Two men–"

"No, Leonora."

"What do you mean, 'no'?"

"No, darling. We . . . that is . . . your mother and I have paid for you to attend a . . . well . . . a sort of program over there."

"WHAT?" I cried, causing Mario and Mr. O. to look over. "A *program*? That's what they said. What type of program? Noooooooo. I don't want to do a program. I want to go to Paris with . . ."

"Boot camp," Daddy interrupted, and this time his voice sounded firm. "We've had enough of your behavior, Leonora. You left us no other option."

A quick replay of their emotional goodbye flashed through my mind. Mommy not asking what I wanted for Christmas dinner. Both of them acting guilty and clingy. Suddenly it all made sense. They had set me up!

No WAAAAAAAAAAAAAAAAAAAAAAAAAAAAAY! cried a voice in my head. "Daddy, I am sooooo *not* staying here. I *won't*. Get me out or send someone to come and get me, and make it SNAPPY."

"It's only for a month," said Daddy.

"No. No. *NOOOO*. What part of that don't you understand?"

"A month, Leonora," Daddy repeated.

"A month? A *month*? Are you out of your mind? It's CHRISTMAS in three weeks! You can't leave me here over Christmas. I . . . you . . . they . . ."

"Goodbye, Leonora. They'll keep us informed of how

you are. And I think you're allowed a letter once a week."

And then he hung up. My own father. Hung up. On me. I couldn't believe it! How DAAAAAAAARE he? I threw down the phone and kicked the wall.

Mario shot me a look as if to say, "Don't do that." *I wouldn't like to get on the wrong side of him*, I thought. *He looks tough*.

Mr. O. was more sympathetic and held up a finger. "One more call," he said.

I scowled at them, picked up the phone from where it had rolled under an old dusty chair, and dialed the only other number that I knew by heart. Tigsy's. She'd get her father to rescue me. He was one of the richest men in Europe. Even richer than my dad. He'd sort it out. And that would show those two losers standing behind me.

The phone rang and rang and rang. *Oh, please pick up, Tigs*, I thought. *Please don't let it go straight to voice mail*.

I was about to give up and try calling Daddy back when she answered. "Hello. Tigsy Piggott's phone."

"Tigs, thank God, listen—"

"Hey, Leonora. Where were you? Where *are* you? Daddy and I went out to get you but were told that the plane had been diverted. Then there was a message from your parents saying that plans had changed. What's going on?"

I turned away from the reception area, from where

40

my two captors were still watching me. "Don't talk, listen," I whispered into the phone. "I've been . . . I'm in a . . ." For a second I wasn't sure what to say. I didn't want to admit that my *own* parents might have really sent me to boot camp. "I . . . I've been kidnapped."

Tigsy burst out laughing. "Oh, Lee-lee! You're such a scream. Kidnapped? Come on, where are you really?"

"That's just it. I don't know. In this place. It might be a hotel, but I think it might some kind of prison. It's cold and spooky. I don't like–"

"Oh, you're *such* a drama queen when you don't like somewhere," said Tigsy. "That's what you said about our room at school, remember? But, actually, I feel the same about this place. People may say that it's the best hotel in Paris, and I know Daddy paid a fortune for us to stay here, but it looks like a prison to me too. Like, I only have four pillows, and you know I like six. So when are you getting here? It will be so much more fun when you're here too. We can play prisoners and escape together!"

"No. Tigs. I'm serious!"

Suddenly the line went crackly.

"What was that? You're breaking up. Bad line. Can you hear me?"

"Tigs. I'm serious. Get help!"

"Can't hear you. I heard 'I'm . . .' *I'm* what?"

"Tigsy, get the call traced. Help!"

"Nope. Can't hear a thing. You're gone. Call me again in five."

"Nooooooooooooooooooo . . . I don't get another call . . . Don't go."

"Later."

And she hung up!

I turned around to face my captors. Mr. O. smiled and gave me the thumbs-up. Mario looked at me as if I was a worm that had just crawled in from the garden. *Oh, no*, I thought. *I just landed in it.*

It's probably best to play along until I know exactly what I'm up against, I decided, as Mr. O. gave me the guided tour of the lodge in his best TV host's manner. *Then I'll plan my escape.*

"What is this building, exactly?" I asked as we toured a maze of dingy corridors. They all looked the same—beige wallpaper on the walls, worn-out green-and-black plaid carpet on the floor, and dim lighting from fixtures on the ceiling that looked like they hadn't been dusted in 100 years. I could see the bodies of dead flies and moths in the bowls of a few of them. And the whole place had the lingering smell of boiled cabbage and lavender furniture polish that reminded me of one of the boarding schools I'd been to. "And where are all the guests?"

"*Guests?* Ha! Oh, you'll meet them soon enough, although I wouldn't exactly call them guests."

"So what is this place, then?"

"Used to be a hotel with a fancy restaurant," said Mr. O., "but since it's a little out of the way, it wasn't doing any business."

"So what is it, then?" I asked again.

"Perfect location for a boot camp. The building was auctioned off in the summer, and a few of us pitched in and got it."

"Why is it the perfect location?" I asked, although I had pretty well figured out the answer.

"It's so out of the way," he replied, and then he laughed and said in a spooky voice. "No one can hear you scream."

Play it very cool, I told myself as a shiver went down my spine. *Very cool.*

"Only joking," said Mr. O. "No need to look so scared. Among other things, I'm an actor, you know." He smiled his bright smile.

I scowled back at him. "I wouldn't give up the day job if I was you. You don't scare me with your silly, scary voice."

"Well! You *are* a rude girl."

I shrugged. "So? Get over it. Maybe someone will take pity on you and give you a job as an extra in some movie that goes straight to DVD."

Mr. O. pursed his lips together. I knew that I'd hit a nerve. *Ha. One to me*, I thought, as he continued the tour and showed me a scruffy gym with some prehistoric-looking workout equipment, a dusty library that looked like it needed some books, since most of the shelves were empty, a huge, dark kitchen at the back of the building that stank of bleach and onions, and a dining room next to it with a long, wooden table and benches in the middle. The whole place appeared shabby and uninhabited, which was what gave it that cold, spooky feeling.

"That kitchen looks unused, and it stinks," I said, as we made our way down yet another corridor.

"Yep. It's hardly been used since the place was a hotel, but that's all changed now. Hermie goes and gets what we need."

"*Hermie?* Who's Hermie?"

"He's in here," said Mr. O. as he opened a door at the end of one of the corridors. "This is the . . . um, the staff room."

It was like walking into a miniature planetarium. Gentle music played from unseen speakers, and it was warm with a lovely smell of baked apples and cinnamon, in contrast to the rest of the lodge. A large mobile of Earth and the surrounding planets hung from a beam that ran along the center of the ceiling. There were posters of the constellations and galaxies on the walls and a painting of the signs of the zodiac. Four comfy-looking armchairs were placed around a roaring fire, and sitting in the chairs were four people who were all staring at me. They seemed like an odd-looking group. First was an old man with a white beard, wearing a tweed suit, who looked like he belonged in a bygone age.

"Dr. Cronus," said Mr. O. "He'll be supervising your lessons."

"*Lessons?*" I asked, as the bearded man gave me a curt nod. He didn't look friendly at all. "Like school?"

"Not exactly. More like karma," said Mr. O. "You know—the theory that as you sow, so you shall reap. That's one of life's biggest lessons."

"Whatever," I said and stifled a yawn.

Next to Dr. Cronus was an extraordinary-looking woman who looked around 30. She had long, silver hair and the appearance of a mermaid without a tail. She had a dreamy expression in her pale eyes and was dressed in green-and-silver clothes that had a hippie feel to them. *So last decade*, I thought, as she glanced over and smiled at me.

"Selene Luna," continued Mr. O. "She'll be your counselor and nurse."

I nodded at her. *Yeah, right*, I told myself. *Play along, play along, keep grinning. Don't let them know that they've got me worried.*

The third person was Mario, and I'd already met him. He didn't even glance up at me.

"You can call him War Bear," said Mr. O. "And, if

you would like to, you can call Selene Mother Moon."

"What's with the wacky names?" I asked.

Mr. O. beamed his smile. "It's what people do at boot camp. I've seen it on TV. All of the organizers and directors have special names. Mine will be . . . um . . . let me think . . . um . . ."

"How about Dingbat Brain?"

Mr. O. actually considered it and then shook his head. "No. No. Not right. Instead you can call me . . . Sun Bird."

"I think I'll stick with Mr. O., if you don't mind," I replied. "You might live in wacko city, but I don't."

The fourth person was the most interesting-looking, and for a brief second I forgot my fear. He was a boy babe straight out of a Calvin Klein commercial. Cute; great, dark, wavy hair to his shoulders; and, like Mario and Mr. O., the same handsome, chiseled features. I immediately felt more cheerful because I like boys, although this one looked at least 19, which is a little too old for me. He turned and gave me the same bright smile as Mr. O. *Must be family,* I thought. *There's something about them all that's similar—although I can't quite put my finger on it. Something in the eyes.*

"Welcome," he said.

"I won't be staying," I replied.

"This is Hermie," said Mr. O. "He's in charge of communication."

"And your name is? Big Bear? Small Bear? Furry Bear?"

Hermie chuckled. "Hey, she's funny," he said to Mr. O. "No. Although some people call me Mercury, you can call me Hermie here. I'll stick with that."

"No. You *have* to have a name," said Mr. O. "Come on. Play the game. Pick a name. The rest of us have."

I glanced over at Mr. O. For a moment there, he had sounded petulant. As if he didn't like not getting his way. *A little like me*, I thought.

"Oh, all right," said Hermie. "I will be . . . Messenger Bear."

Mr. O. looked appeased. "Hmm. That's okay, I suppose. You have her phone for her?"

Hermie nodded and reached into a desk behind him.

Phone? I asked myself. *These idiots are going to actually let me have a phone?*

Hermie tossed me a package wrapped in gold paper, and everyone watched me unwrap it as if it was gift-giving time at Christmas.

I ripped off the last strip of paper. Inside *was* a phone and a small box. The phone was gold with a single and very large diamond at the top above the numbers. *Tacky*, I thought. It didn't look cheap, but it wasn't exactly the height of sophistication, either. The assorted crazies, however, were looking at me like I'd just won the lottery. *They really are insane*, I thought. *First they kidnap*

47

me, and then they give me a phone. Like, duh. Do they think that I won't actually use it to call for help?

"You can use it to get in touch with me whenever you want to," said Mr. O., beaming.

"You? And why would I want to do that when you're right here in the same place as me?"

Mr. O. tapped the side of his nose. "Ah, but who knows what the next month holds? You might get lost while out on a hike. You might need to talk to someone. Oh, yes, I think you'll find that you come to value that phone dearly."

"And I think *you'll* find that, even if I did need to talk to someone, you'd be the last person on Earth. What makes you think that I would want to talk to you?"

"Because I am your guardian!" said Mr. O.

I rolled my eyes. "Whatever," I said with a sigh. I put the phone to one side and opened the box. Inside was a white-gold chain with a charm on it. I looked more closely and saw that the charm was a tiny lion's head.

"The lion for a Leo," said Mr. O. "Only very *special* people get these phones and a necklace like that, and you have been chosen to join their ranks."

I tossed the phone and necklace aside. "Yeah. Yeah. Whatever."

Mr. O. flushed red and looked like he was going to explode. I could see that a vein on his forehead was throbbing. "Well! You *spoiled* little brat!"

Mario took Mr. O. aside and was talking to him as if he was trying to calm him down. *But what's the big deal?* I asked myself. At home I have five cell phones and a whole drawer full of jewelry. No way was I impressed by these pathetic little trinkets that looked like they came out of a cheap quarter machine.

Mr. O. turned back to the room. "Hermie, give her the papers," he said.

Hermie reached inside the desk, and this time he pulled out a pile of papers that he handed to me.

I glanced down. The first page had what looked like a geometric drawing on it. A circle with squares and lines all over it.

"It's your horoscope," said Mr. O.

"So? Big deal. I already know my horoscope. Mommy has a private astrologer, and he did my chart when I was a baby. He gives us updates every month."

"In that case, you'll know that you have some SEVERE lessons coming up," said Dr. Cronus.

I stuck my tongue out at him.

He rolled his eyes up to the heavens. "Childish," he said, and Mr. O. nodded enthusiastically in agreement. "Should have known you'd respond like that. It's all in your chart. Childish. Spoiled. Stubborn. Used to having your own way. We need to put up some boundaries. Honestly, Leos. They all think that the world revolves around them. Always the same. And you're a Leo with

Leo rising and the Moon in Gemini."

"So?"

"The Moon in Gemini means that you have a short attention span," said Selene.

"And you're a double Leo. A real handful," said Mr. O.

"And Mars in Taurus at the time of your birth, which can make you willful and stubborn if you don't get your own way," said Mario with a shake of his head.

"Indeed. You have a thing or two to learn, all right," said Dr. Cronus, and then he seemed to lose interest and turned back to the fire. "Still. All in good time."

Mr. O. reached over and took the papers from my hand. "One thing that your astrologer *didn't* tell you and that is, according to the stars, you are this month's Zodiac Girl. That's the real news!" At this point, all of the people in the room nodded, albeit wearily in the doctor's case.

Mr. O. waited to see my reaction, and I had a feeling that I was supposed to have fallen to the floor in amazement and kissed his feet. As it was, I was distinctly underwhelmed.

"Yeah? So?"

"I am saying that you are a Zodiac Girl," he repeated.

"Which means what, exactly?"

"It means that, for one month, you get the help of me and my companions here."

"Like a special offer at the supermarket? I think I'll

pass, thank you very much."

Dr. Cronus tutted his disapproval loudly, and Mr. O. looked very, *very* angry.

"Millions of girls would kill to be in your position," he said.

"Cool, so let them come here and be a *Zodiac Girl* and let me go home or to Paris, which is where I'm supposed to be."

Everyone who was gathered muttered more disapproval when I said this.

Mr. O. threw my horoscope up in the air. "I am clearly wasting my time here!" He looked dangerously close to having a tantrum. "I don't think that you understand, Leonora," he said through gritted teeth. "To be chosen as a Zodiac Girl is a rare honor."

"Okay, so what do you get as Zodiac Girl? A tiara? A sash? A trophy? There's only one thing I want right now and that is the fastest way possible out of here."

"You'll get a good whipping if I have my way," said Dr. Cronus.

Selene got up and came over to Mr. O. "Now, now," she soothed. "That's not the attitude. She is a child."

"*A child!* No. I'm not. Go on," I goaded. "Let me have it. Come on, see if I care." I'd dealt with worse old loons than him and Dr. Cronus in my time. "But I have to warn you, if you lay one finger on me, I'll sue. My father has the best lawyers—"

"Zip it, zit girl," said Dr. Cronus.

Zit girl! I put my hand up to my forehead where I'd covered up my zits that morning. My concealer must have worn off. "Buh . . . wuh . . ." I blustered. The old Crony had actually called me *zit girl*, and now he was snickering with Mr. O. as if they were ten-year-old boys who'd just made a really good joke. *How rude!*

Mr. O. composed himself and then shook his head. "No, no, you're not getting it, Leonora. You have the aid of the stars for one month. Don't you see how wonderful that is?"

I raised an eyebrow at him as if to say that no, I didn't.

"It's true," he said. "I am the Sun, Selene is the Moon, Hermie is Hermes, otherwise known as Mercury, Dr. Cronus is Saturn, and Mario is no less than Mars himself."

Oh. My. God. I'd been captured by a bunch of lunatics. I'd had enough. "Yeah, yeah, yeah. And I'm the queen of Sheba," I said as I grabbed the zodiac phone and made a dash for the door.

Chapter Five
No escape

I ran down the maze of corridors, not sure where I was going or what I was going to do. All I knew was that I had to get away. I ran through the empty kitchen and tried the back door. It was locked with three enormous brass bolts and no sign of a key, so I looked in all of the nearby drawers, pots, and jars.

I ran back through to the front and tried the door there. It was also locked. *Weird that no one's coming after me*, I thought, as I glanced down at the zodiac phone, punched in Tigsy's number, and waited to hear it ring. Nothing. Maybe there was no signal in such a remote place. And then the phone rang. I pressed a button that was flashing green and listened.

"Hey, kid," said Mr. O.'s voice. "Just checking that it's working."

"I can't call out on it. I just tried it."

"Oh, it's not for calling out to anybody. Do you think we were born yesterday?" In the background I could hear laughter when he said this. "It's for you and me to keep in touch. I'm your zodiac guardian, remember?"

53

"Oh, really. You and me?"

"Yeah."

"*Just* you and me?"

"And maybe the other planets that I introduced you to, should you need them."

I chose to ignore the "other planets" issue. "But I can't use it to call out? Or receive calls from outside?"

"Nope."

"Oh, really. Hmm. Well, I'll show you exactly what I think about that," I said and threw down the phone onto the floor and then stomped on it over and over until it was just a pile of splintered gold particles.

"You're going to regret that," said Mr. O.'s voice from the splinters. "You have the Moon and Mars in your—"

I stomped on the phone again.

"Drama queen!" said his voice again. "Throwing tantrums is no way to get through life, you know. All I wanted to tell you was that it's a new moon tonight, so things might get . . ."

And then the phone made a fizzing sound, a pop, and then it went quiet.

Things might get what? I wondered as I ran back down the corridors and up onto the second floor, which was deserted, and all of the doors were locked, with no sign of a fire escape anywhere. It was also strange that no one had tried to follow me. I ran back downstairs and had stopped to catch my breath when the mermaid-looking lady came strolling toward me. She smiled and then pointed to my right. "Down there and to the left."

And off she went.

What did she mean? What was down there? A way out? More lunatics who thought that they were planets? Dinner? What? Thinking about dinner made me realize that I was hungry, *starving*, in fact. *But where is the staff in this place?* I wondered. *Where are the waitresses and waiters? And where's my suite? In fact, maybe I'll put off running away until the morning when I've had a good night's sleep. If Mommy and Daddy have paid, then the facilities are bound to be okay, since we never stay anywhere that's less than five stars.*

I decided that I had nothing to lose by following Selene's directions and was about to set off when Hermie appeared. *Now, who is he again?* I asked myself. *What did Mr. O. say? That Hermie was the delivery boy or the messenger or something?*

"Where's my suite?" I asked. "And I'd like a chocolate milk shake and some French fries brought in. Mr. O. said you're the one who gets what we need?"

Hermie cracked up laughing. "*Suite?* How should I know? I am Mercury, the planet of communication."

"So *communicate.* Tell me where my room is and then get me a milk shake."

Hermie cracked up again and bowed. "Right. Chocolate milk shake? French fries? I'll see what I can do."

"Thanks," I said. "And be quick about it."

"Sure. Quick is my specialty, actually. I can be as quick as if I had winged feet sometimes," he said and then winked. "In the meantime, you need to go down to the door on your left. It's time to sign in."

"You mean to get my suite?"

Hermie nodded. "Yeah. To . . . get your suite."

I turned and made my way to the room that he'd indicated. I opened the door, and there was Selene behind a table with a pile of clothes on it. "How did you get in here?" I asked. I'd only just seen her a few moments ago, walking the other way.

She tapped the side of her nose. "The Moon has many mysteries, many secrets," she said, and she picked up a pile of clothes, a pair of sneakers, a black baseball cap, and a small brown paper bag from the table and handed them to me. "Now, first things first. You've missed dinner, so here's a sandwich, an apple, and a box of orange juice."

I peeked in the bag and handed it back to Selene. "Um, no. I don't think so. I only eat red apples, and that one is green. I don't eat whole-wheat bread, I only like ciabatta—toasted—and I *don't* do orange juice. I've already ordered some fries and a milk shake."

Selene took back the bag. "Are you sure? You must be hungry."

"I'd rather eat my own arm than that."

"Suit yourself," said Selene. "You might actually have to do that. But in the meantime, you have to change. When in boot camp, you have to dress like a boot camper. So, off with those clothes you've got on, and put these on."

I glanced at the clothes that she'd given me. A navy polar fleece top, sweatpants, and a pair of plain white sneakers. Off the scale of even uncool. The sneakers weren't even by a *cheap* designer. "Are you out of your mind?"

"So some folks say," she replied. "I am the Moo—"

"Yeah, yeah. I heard Mr. O.'s intro. You're the Moon. Good for you. And I'm a teapot. Yeah. We've been through the introductions. So. Where are my things and my suitcase?"

Selene looked taken aback. "In the storeroom. You can have them back at the end."

"End? But . . . you *can't* take away my things. They're mine."

She gave me a simpering smile. "Not anymore," she said and then held out a transparent plastic bag. "Now put your jewelry in here."

I put my hand up to my throat and touched my locket on its silver chain. A ripple of panic went through me. "No. *No.* I can't do that. I *won't* do that."

Selene smiled again. "We don't use the word 'won't' here. Nor 'can't.' " In a second her expression changed and became sad. "Now hand over the jewelry." She held out her hand.

I wasn't actually wearing that much jewelry, only my studs, my locket and chain, and my silver bracelet. None of it was worth very much, since I tend not to travel in my valuable stuff, but there was no way that I would be handing it over, especially not the locket. "No," I said. "You can take a hike." I noticed that she was wearing a necklace. It was a pendant with a circle in the middle and two half moons on each side. "You have on a necklace, so I'm going to keep mine."

Selene looked alarmed, like she was going to cry. "A hike at this time of night? No. Oh. Don't be difficult. I do so hate it when people don't cooperate. It can make me very *emotional*! And especially when there's a new moon in the sky like there is tonight. It's a time for new beginnings, you know. A *good* time if you give it a chance and don't resist it. It can be a time for rejuvenation. So don't make me MAD! Lunatics, they're MAD, aren't they? Lune. *Another* word for Moon. Making sense now, is it? Moon. Lune, loon. So I'm warning you—I can get *MAD*."

I jumped back when she shouted the word "mad," since she said it with such force. *Boy, Mr. O. said this lady was a counselor, but she's clearly way unstable*, I thought as I headed for the door.

"MARIO!" Selene called, and in an instant Mario

appeared and blocked my way out. "Leonora doesn't want to hand over her jewelry."

Mario gave her a curt nod. "It's the rules," he said, and then he strode over and bent down so that we were nose to nose. "Now hand it over, or else you and I are going to stand here all night."

I crossed my arms and shut my eyes. "Fine."

Seconds went by, and I took a peek. He hadn't budged an inch. His big face loomed in front of me. We were almost eyeball to eyeball. At my last school, I could outstare anyone, but this guy was out of my league. I quickly shut my eyes again. *Out of sight, out of mind*, I thought.

Minutes went by, and I took another peek. He hadn't budged.

"I'd give up now if I was you," Selene advised. "He can stay like that for decades."

"I am *not* going to give you my jewelry," I said.

"Yes, you are, missy. Everyone else does. Studs, piercings, bracelets, and beads. All in the bag."

"They're not worth anything. Honest. I have much more expensive jewelry at home, and you're welcome to that, just . . . *please* don't make me take off my locket."

"And what's so special about the chain?" asked Selene.

I really didn't want to talk about it. I didn't talk to anyone about it. I didn't talk about any of my real feelings or fears. Not anymore. I hadn't for a long time.

"Nothing. Just I . . . I always wear it."

"And now it's time to hand it over," said Mario.

"No. Look," I said as I slipped off my bracelet and took out my studs. "You can have these. Come on. Meet me halfway. I'm cooperating."

Mario took the jewelry that I handed him and put it in the bag and then looked back at me. "Now give me the locket," he said.

"*No.*" I felt a rising panic at the thought of being without it. "And you can't bully me."

"Not bullying you, missy. Those are the rules. Now come on—what's so special about that locket?"

I pushed the feeling of panic away. Down deep inside. I wasn't going to let him know that I felt intimidated. I'd learned that lesson long ago with Poppy. Never let them see how scared you are. "My sister gave it to me."

"And you'll get it back at the end of the program. Now hand it over."

"No. No. NOOOOOOOOOOOOOOOOOOOO." I lashed out at him with my arms and went to kick him, but he stepped back in the nick of time. Instead my foot crashed into the wall.

"OWWWWWW! Oo-oo. OWWWWW. And now you've made me hurt myself. I HATE you. You're HORRIBLE!" I yelled. *They could never understand about Poppy and me*, I thought. *Why should they?* "And I'm NOT getting changed into those clothes either. I mean, navy? Hello? *So* last decade."

I wanted to throw an almighty tantrum but got the feeling that I'd gone far enough and that a mega tantrum wouldn't play here. I also felt like I was going to cry. I started to shiver, and Selene looked over at me with a sympathetic expression on her face. "Okay, look, Leonora," she said, "I'll cut you some slack since this is your first night. You put on the clothes, and you can keep on the locket. How about that?"

My first instinct was to tell her to shove it, but it was late. I wanted my chocolate milk shake and fries. I wanted to go to bed and get some sleep. I wanted these crazy people off my back. I nodded. "Okay. But ask him to leave."

"I'm leaving," said Mario. "Don't worry."

And off he went.

"Good girl," said Selene as I picked up the clothes. She handed me a cup of what looked like water. "Now drink this water."

"Water? With nothing to flavor it?"

Selene nodded. "It's all you're getting."

"Okay, but is it *Evian*? That's the brand I drink."

Selene gave me a "Don't be so stupid" look. I took that as a no, so I took the cup and drank, but only because I was about to die of thirst, or else I wouldn't have touched the stuff.

"Good girl," she said again.

I turned my back on her. She annoyed me. They *all* annoyed me. I wasn't a good girl. I knew I was bad. I took off my clothes and put on my prison outfit. I was exhausted, but tomorrow, *tomorrow*, she was going to see just how difficult I could be. And so were the rest of them. "Okay. So, please, can I go to my room now?"

"Sure," she said. "Follow me."

Chapter Six

The others

"No. This can't be right," I said, as I looked around the dingy, narrow room that Selene took me to. With the windows so high that you'd need to stand on a chair to look out of them, it really did resemble a prison. Where was my private room? My bed? My bags? All I could see was this unwelcoming dorm with three twin beds on one side. No pictures. No flowers. No bowls of fruit or a TV. No phone. No Evian. No *nothing*. Just beds, bare cream walls, and a couple of sets of drawers and a wardrobe. And it felt damp. I could see condensation on the windows and the glisten of moisture on the shiny wall just beneath it.

Selene pointed at the bed that was farthest away on the right. "That's where you'll be sleeping."

"But . . . but it's not even made up!" I said, as I took in the blanket, bedspread, and sheet that were in a neat pile on the end of the bed. "And where are the pillows?"

"You have to earn those," said Selene.

"Wha—?!" I was so stunned, I couldn't think of anything to say. To think that MY mother and father had sent me here. I felt a rage inside like I'd never experienced before and was aware that my jaw had tightened, my fists had clenched, and I had a bitter taste at the back of my mouth. How DARE they? Even though I had no doubt that I'd be out tomorrow, to even leave me here for *one* night was unjust. Completely terrible. I was going to so make them suffer when I got home. In fact, I'd take them to court. I would sue them for unreasonable behavior. I would sell my sad story to the papers to the highest bidder, and that way I'd be financially free of them. Then I would leave home. Go and live with Tigsy. That would show them. No. Maybe not. They'd probably like that. Out of sight, out of mind. I didn't think they really loved me anymore, so they'd be glad to get rid of me. I was a constant reminder of Poppy and what had happened, so they'd probably be happier if I left. So, no. I'd stay and make their life miserable.

"So, I'll leave you to it," said Selene. "You can make your bed, and then the others will be back soon from their hike, and you can meet them after their dinner."

I still couldn't speak. I pinched myself. Surely I'd fallen asleep on the plane and was having a nightmare? This *couldn't* be happening for real. I was Leonora Hedley-Dent. Daughter of Alex and Clara Hedley-Dent. We were loaded. We stayed in the types of places that most people dreamed about. Places that were among the best mega-luxury, seven-star locations on the planet. Not dingy dives in Loserville like this dump. So Mom and Dad didn't like me. So what? I still always got my own way. I did. Did. Did. Did. Did. Surely Mom and Dad couldn't hate me this much? I bent over, pulled at the blanket on the bed closest to me, and yanked it off.

"Um . . . Marilyn's not going to like that," said Selene.

"Never mind Marilyn. Who's she anyway? Actually, don't answer. I don't care. I've met enough deadbeat losers for one day. And you know what? Leonora doesn't LIKE IT!" I shouted and then proceeded to pull the blankets off *all* the beds, shove them on the floor, and then stomp on them. Selene didn't attempt to stop me. In fact, she didn't seem bothered at all. She just waited until I'd stripped every bed bare and then said, "Okay. Feel better now?"

"No, I DON'T!" I yelled and made my way down to my bed, lay face-down, and thrashed away with my arms and legs.

As I wailed into the mattress, I heard the door open and close.

"Ah, a new girl," said a female voice.

"Yeah, and see what the stupid fool has done to my bed," said a second voice in a cockney English accent.

Fool, I thought. *Did someone just call ME a fool?* I stopped mid-wail and tilted my head so that I could see who had come in. Two girls were standing at the other end of the room staring at me. Both were medium height—one with dark, wavy, shoulder-length hair and glasses and the other with long, blonde hair and a wide mouth. *Older than me*, I decided. *Maybe 17?* The blonde one was wearing a tank top, even though it was cold in the room, and she had a tattoo on her upper right arm. *Tattoos are so has-been rock star*, I thought, *but I suppose she thinks that it makes her look tough.*

"Right, introductions," said Selene cheerfully. *She really is deranged*, I thought. *Like I'd ever want to meet these two.* "Now. This is Marilyn Brocklehurst and Lynn Bailey. Girls, meet Leonora Hedley-Dent."

The dark-haired girl named Marilyn scowled at me. "'edley-Bent, is it? Hey, you, posh girl. You responsible for messing up my bed?"

Her friend snickered and watched to see what I was going to do. I turned away.

"Hey, 'edley-Bent," repeated Marilyn. "I wanna lie down."

I decided I was going to show them that they didn't intimidate me, so I sat up and looked over at them. "Then get one of the staff to do it," I said.

Lynn snorted with laughter, and I saw Selene slink away and close the door behind her. *Oh, God*, I thought. *She's left me alone with them.* Marilyn fixed her eyes on me, clenched her fists, and approached. I took a sharp intake of breath and braced myself for a beating.

However, just as Marilyn got close, she slumped down on the bed next to mine.

"What you in for, then?" she asked.

I felt torn. Part of me didn't want to talk to anyone. Another part wanted to know what was going on. Where I was. What the program was all about. That part won. "Nothing. It's all been a huge mistake. I'll be out of here in the morning."

Both girls burst out laughing, like I'd said the funniest thing ever, and Lynn came to sit next to Marilyn. "That's what we said too, when we got here," she said. "All a big mistake."

"Okay. So what are you in for?" I asked.

Marilyn narrowed her eyes and jutted her chin forward. "Murder. Di'n't like one of my teachers, so I snuffed 'im out one night down a back alley."

I cracked up laughing. "Yeah, right. Do I look like I was born yesterday?"

Marilyn looked annoyed. "Yeah, you do, actually. And you'll get it too, if you don't watch it."

I laughed again, which I could see annoyed Marilyn even more, but I was sure that she was just trying to scare me, and I was determined to show that I wasn't frightened in the least. "So, what are you really in for?"

"None of your business. You ask too many questions," said Marilyn, who got up and slouched away.

"So, what about you?" I asked Lynn.

"*So, what about you?*" Marilyn mimicked in a posh voice from behind her. I ignored her.

"Yeah. Me, too. Um . . . murder," said Lynn.

I rolled my eyes. "Can't you think of your own dumb answer?" I said.

"Okay, yeah. I'm in for drinking."

"*Drinking?*"

"Yeah. Wine. Baileys. Crème de menthe. I like to drink. Christmas liqueurs are my favorite, but . . . I'm warning you—they have a funny effect sometimes. I don't know what I'm doing. They send me a bit . . ." She made a circle in the air near her temple with her finger and made her eyes cross. ". . . demented. People say it's chemical, like, but, whatever."

Behind her, Marilyn chuckled.

"Yeah. 'Course," I said wearily, as if I'd heard it all a million times. "*Chemical.* Whatever."

Marilyn began mimicking the way I spoke again. "Yeah. 'Course. Chemicaaaal," she said in her infuriating version of a posh accent.

"I do *not* speak like that," I said.

"Ay do not spake like thaaat," she repeated.

I got up off the bed and moved away. Already I wished that I'd kept my zodiac phone. Okay, so I could only reach Mr. O., but even he was better than these two psychos. Although I could tell that they weren't murderers and were putting on the tough act, I wasn't sure what the real story was, and, until I was, I thought it was best not to push them too far, especially since there were two of them against me.

"Yeah, you do sound stuck-up," said Lynn. "Just remember—when we don't like someone, we do away with them, so you'd better watch yer back, Smedley-Pent."

I turned back to them. "Hedley-Dent," I said. "If you're going to say my name, say it correctly. And you don't scare me. So kill me. See if I care."

Marilyn raised an eyebrow, came back up the aisle, and put her face very close to mine, not unlike the way that Mario had before, when I said I wouldn't take off my jewelry. Up close, she smelled like peppermint. This time, I didn't close my eyes, and I made myself stare back at her. For a moment, my chest tightened— I thought that she really was going to pound me this time—but she didn't.

"Later," she said and then walked back up to the other end of the room.

Later what? Is she going to kill me in my sleep? I wondered as the door opened and two boys came in. One was dark, tall, and lanky with slouched shoulders and a pinched expression on his face. The other short one had red hair tied back in a ponytail and a friendly face. They surveyed the mess on the floor and then looked accusingly at me. I did a half-lip snarl back at them to show them that I was tough and not to be messed with.

"You're *not* telling me that we share with boys?" I asked.

Lynn shook her head. "No, they're in the dorm next door, thank God. Mark and Jake. Meet our new princess."

I gave them a royal wave to let them know that I wasn't intimidated by them either. The dark-haired one shrugged and turned away, while the red-haired one knelt on the floor and starting howling like a dog.

"Cut it out, Jake," said Marilyn. "No need to keep up the act in 'ere when it's just us."

This nightmare just gets worse and worse, I thought, as I glanced over at Lynn and hoped for an explanation.

"Jake's playing the crazy card," she said.

"*Crazy card?*"

"Yeah, he's hoping that by acting insane, he might be sent home."

Good idea, Jake, I thought. *I should have thought of that.* I looked over at Mark, who had gone over to the window and was staring out into the black night.

"And Mark has taken a vow of silence," said Lynn. "Hasn't spoken for over a week now."

"A *week!* You guys have been here a week?"

Lynn nodded.

By the window, Mark had pulled a little notebook out of his pocket and was writing something. When he'd finished, he came over and held up the paper in front of me.

70

Keep out of my way, and I'll keep out of yours. If not, you're dead.

"Oh, how sweet, another threat on my life," I gushed. "And sooooo nice to meet you too . . . loser." I stuck my tongue out at him. He scowled at me and went back to the window.

Selene popped her head around the door. "Lights out in five. Boys, back to your dorm," she said and then disappeared again.

"But I haven't eaten anything, and I'm HUNGRY," I yelled after her.

Selene's hand appeared around the door and dumped a paper bag onto the floor. It was the bag that contained the apple and the sandwich that she'd given me earlier.

"No WAAAAAAAAAAAAY!" I yelled. "What part of 'NOOOOOOO WAAAAY' don't you understand?"

Mark, Jake, Lynn, and Marilyn all seemed highly amused when the same arm appeared around the door, a little lower this time, and took back the bag.

"No luck," said Marilyn. "I would 'ave 'ad that."

The boys left the dorm, and, two minutes later, the lights did go out.

I sat in the dark for a moment and could hear Lynn and Marilyn getting into their beds.

"Um, girls . . ." I said. "Um . . . has anyone said anything about you being Zodiac Girls or anything about planets being here in physical form . . . ?" I trailed off because it sounded insane.

"No. Why?" replied Lynn. "What are you talking about? You're crazy, you are."

"Oh, nothing. Forget it," I said. *Maybe the planet nonsense is a special type of torture that they're saving just for me,* I thought, as I groped my way to the bottom of the bed, grabbed the blanket, and snuggled under it. I kept the horrible clothes on because I was freezing.

As I lay there and stared into the dark room, my mind played over the past couple of hours. It had been unreal. All that nonsense about me being a Zodiac Girl. *What was that about?* I thought as my stomach growled. Mr. O. kept saying that it was a rare honor. *Honestly! A rare honor to be put through this mortification, and no dinner, either? If this is a rare honor, Mr. O. can shove it where the sun don't shine. This has to be the second-worst day of my whole life.*

I closed my eyes and tried to shut out the nightmare scenario. I was starving, and I'd never felt so lonely. I was also beginning to get the feeling that there wasn't going to be any room service bringing my fries and milk shake.

Chapter Seven
Wake-up call

"Tah tah tat ta TAAAAAAAAAAAAAAAAAAAAA."

It seemed as if I had only just closed my eyes when a *horrible* noise blasted into the room. Like someone was playing a very LOUD trumpet a quarter of an inch away from my right ear. I woke up with a jolt. I wasn't sure where I was. For one gorgeous second, I'd imagined that I was back in my room in St. Kitts. Coco curled up on the end of my bed. Staff on hand outside to carry out my every whim. But, no. It was dark in the room, and I felt confused. It didn't smell like home. It smelled like . . . boiled onions and bleach with a trace of peppermint.

A light came on. A *very* bright overhead light. And all illusions were shattered as the previous day came back to me. I was in hell with a bunch of losers, and our captors were psychos who thought that they were living embodiments of the planets.

"OhmigooooooooOOOOOOOOOOD," I groaned. "This caaaaaaan't be haaaaappeniiiiiiiing."

"It can and it is. So zip it, posh girl," said Marilyn, as

she blinked sleepily in the next bed. "It's bad enough 'ere without you whining."

Next to her, Lynn moaned. "I haaaate mornings," she said.

Marilyn stumbled out of bed with a scowl on her face. I looked at my watch and saw that it was 5:30 in the morning. I'd never in my life been up at that time! I snuggled farther down into the bed. They'd have to drag me out if they wanted to get me up. For one thing, it was so cold in the room that I could see my own breath, and, for another, now that I'd slept a little, I felt my fighting spirit return, and I had to plan out my course of action.

My fellow inmates fell out of their beds and out the door, which surprised me, since neither of them had seemed like pussycats the night before.

"Where are you going?" I called to Lynn.

"Bathroom, then breakfast, then chores."

"Hmm. Sounds like a fun day. NOOOOOOT. So. To get up and join you or not to get up? Hmm. What a difficult decision. Um . . . turn off the light when you go, Lynn, and ask one of the psychos to bring me a cup of hot chocolate in a couple of hours."

Lynn curtsied. "Why, sure, your royal highness," she said, "and I'll ask them to turn up the heating, too, should I?"

"Oh, yeah. Would you? I'm amazed that we didn't

all die of hypothermia during the night."

I turned over, and, when she didn't turn off the light, I pulled the blanket farther over my head. As I did, I noticed a note written on bright yellow paper flutter onto the floor. I picked it up and glanced at it.

Mars is in Capricorn at the moment, and Saturn is in Aquarius (that's Mario and Dr. Cronus, in case you weren't listening yesterday, Leonora). The day will start with an intense confrontation that you could learn from. Back down if you have any sense. And the Moon may bring up some painful memories. Remember that what you resist persists. Bye for now, kiss kiss, your guardian, Mr. O. (a.k.a. the Sun).

"The confrontation starts with you, saddo," I said, as I ripped it up into little pieces. "And I'm not backing down."

A few minutes later, I heard footsteps and someone yanked off the blanket. It was Mario. He was standing at the end of the bed, legs astride, hands on his hips.

"Hey! Do you mind?" I said, as I grabbed for the top of the blanket and tried to pull it back over me. "It's like a fridge in here."

Mario looked at his watch. "You've got ten seconds."

"Yeah, yeah, whatever," I said as I lay back down and turned away.

"Ten . . . nine . . . eight . . . seven . . . six . . . better get up, missy . . . four . . ."

"Or else what?"

"No breakfast."

"Ooh, like I care," I said, but actually I felt torn because I was hungry. On the other hand, I didn't want to give in too easily.

"Three . . . two . . ."

I leaped up. "Okay, okay. Keep your hair on."

"Keep your hair on, *sir*. You will address me as 'sir' from now on."

"You have to be kidding. I have never called anyone 'sir' in my life, and I'm not about to start now."

"I'm sure there'll be a lot of things that you've never experienced before that are gonna happen here. Getting up at five-thirty, for a start."

"Yeah, yeah. *Sir*. So what happened to Brother Sun, Sister Moon, and all that garbage?"

"That's for the others. I prefer that you call me 'sir.'"

"Oh, get a life, soldier boy. Now, tell me where to go for breakfast."

A flash of annoyance crossed Mario's face, and I saw him bite his cheek as if he was holding back what he'd really like to say. "I'll tell you where to go, but first you give me some respect, girl."

I did a jerky dance around the bed the way that I'd seen the cool rappers do it on TV, and then I put my forefinger and middle finger together and pointed at the floor. "Okay, my man, get down, get cool. Yo. Respect," I said in my best Busta Rhymes voice.

Mario wasn't impressed. Or amused.

"You know who I am, girl?"

I nodded and did a mock salute. "The planet Mars. Here on Earth. In physical form, SIR!" And then I couldn't help but snicker. I mean, how utterly absurd! If Tigsy was here, we'd both be on the floor laughing our heads off.

Mario scowled. "According to your birth chart, I am here to teach you some respect for others, Miss Hedley-Dent."

I began to do my rapper dance around him again. "Yo, get down . . ."

"Right, that's it," he said. "No breakfast."

I straightened up and stuck out my bottom lip. "Do I care?"

"You will."

I stuck my tongue out at him.

"And that just earned you . . . no lunch either."

I stuck my tongue out at him again.

He turned to go and pointed at the door. "You'll learn. Bathroom out to the right."

After he'd left the room, I ran to the window to see if I could see where I was, but it was still dark outside.

I was bursting to go to the bathroom, so I went in search of one. I knew that I didn't have far to go, because I could hear the sound of water. And screaming.

"What's going on?" I asked when I opened a door and saw Marilyn by the sink.

She jutted her chin toward a door. "Shower. Cold. Lynn lost her hot shower privilege yesterday for talking back."

I couldn't believe what I was hearing. "You have to *earn* hot water?"

"You said it, princess."

"But that's inhumane."

"Innit? But try telling that to Mario," she replied.

Enough, I thought. *I don't care that it's still dark outside. It will be light soon enough.* I quickly used the bathroom, ran back to the dorm, put on my boot-camp sneakers, grabbed the blanket, and wrapped it around myself. It would help keep me warm when I was outside— because I was leaving, and *no one* was going to stop me.

I tiptoed out into the corridor and crept out to the front. Miracle of miracles. The door was open!

I glanced behind me. No one was around, so I opened the door and slipped out. It felt like I'd opened the door of a fridge—it was so cold out there and dark—and far away in the distant sky I could see the Moon. As my eyes grew accustomed to the darkness, I could just about see in front of me. I thought back to what Selene had said last night about the word "lune" meaning crazy. *Yeah, I must be crazy to be doing this, but, whatever, I have just found my inner lunatic,* I thought.

Keeping my back to the wall, I crept along until there was a window. There I fell to my knees so that, if anyone was looking out, they wouldn't see me. I crawled through some shrubs—not easy with the stupid blanket—and down to a path that led through some woods. Along the way, I felt a nail break. *This is just the end!* I thought. *Can things possibly get any worse? I just pray that no one I know ever finds out about this!* Once I'd reached the path, I stood up and looked around. I couldn't see any lights in the distance or sign of habitation at all—just the black silhouette of trees and hills as far as the eye could see. Mr. O. had said that it was remote, but there was *bound* to be something somewhere if I went far enough. There had to be.

A quick glance back to ensure that I hadn't been spotted, and then I headed for the trees.

I ran for around 15 minutes, staying parallel with the path leading away from the boot camp, but I made sure that I was hidden by the trees. *Thank God there's a little bit of light from the Moon*, I thought, as I panted along next to the path, which seemed to go on forever and ever without actually getting anywhere. I cursed the fact that we'd arrived in the dark last night; if it had been daylight, I might have been able to gauge exactly how far I was from people. And from being rescued.

I ran on, stopping for breath every now and then. It didn't look as if anyone was following me, so I slowed down my pace. I so wished that I had eaten that sandwich and apple last night. I was *starving*. *I will probably die soon*, I thought. *Then they'll all be sorry.*

"Starving and with broken nails. Thanks a lot, Mom and Dad!" I yelled at the sky and then realized that maybe that wasn't such a good idea. Someone might have heard me. I thought about all of the candy bars that I'd stashed in my suitcase, and my mouth watered. I was sooooooooo hungry and thirsty. A drop of water splashed down on my face. Another drop. And another. And then the heavens opened up, and it began to rain.

Oh, very funny, God—yeah, add to the fun and make it rain, why don't you? I thought, as I made a dash for shelter under the thickest branches that I could see. But it was no use. It was December, and the trees were bare. The blanket that I had wrapped around me wasn't waterproof, so it was soon heavy with rain. A wave of anger flooded through me. Cold and hungry and thirsty, in the dark, and NOW WET! How *could* my mom and dad *do* this to me? I was going to die. I knew it. I was lost in the forest in the middle of nowhere. Like Little Red Riding Hood. *Oh, God, I hope there aren't wolves around*, I thought. *Oh, God, oh, God. I might get eaten by wild animals, and then crows will come and peck at my carcass. And no one will miss me until it's too late. Mom and Dad think that I'm at the boot camp, tucked up in my bed, not lost in the middle of nowhere. Oh, God. They'll read about my death in the paper.*

Ha! THEN they'll be extra sorry. Oh, yeah.

An image of my funeral flashed through my mind. Tigsy would be there, of course, wearing something fabulous with great big black sunglasses. She'd be followed by Coco, whose fur would have been dyed black for the occasion. My little Coco. She'd miss me. *Oh, what should I do?* I asked myself. I looked to the left, then to the right. In front. *Where should I go? Which way? How long can a person actually last without fries and a milk shake and a decent manicure?*

I dropped to the ground. I so wished that I could talk to Tigsy. Or Poppy. At the thought of Poppy, I felt overwhelmingly sad. She loved me. She really did. She followed me around from the day that she was born. Her big sister. Her hero. And then the very time that she'd needed me the most, I'd let her down. I stood up and slapped my arms to stay warm. *Must not think about her. Must not. Must not. Too, too painful.* And then I wondered if these were the painful feelings that Mr. O. had warned me about in his note, the ones that the Moon would bring up. *No. No way. He couldn't know about my sister or about what I really felt deep, deep inside.*

And then I heard the roar of . . . what was it? Thunder? *Oh, no.* Where there was thunder, there was lightning. I might get struck by it if the storm came closer. But, no. It wasn't thunder. It was . . . I could see a headlight coming up the path. It was a motorcycle.

I made up my mind in an instant. I couldn't stay out here in this weather a moment longer. I'd have to revert to plan B to escape. The fact that I didn't have a plan B was beside the point. I'd come up with one, all in good time. For the moment, though, I needed to get dry.

I hopped out of the trees and flagged down the motorcycle. The rider slowed down and came to a stop. As I approached, I saw that it was the cute boy-babe messenger, Hermie.

"Been running away, have you?" he asked.

I nodded. "Five stars for observation."

He ignored the sarcasm in my voice. "Ready to go back?"

A trickle of rainwater dripped down my forehead and along my nose as I nodded again.

"Hop on," he said.

I did as I was told, and a second later, just as Hermie revved the engine, a man stepped out from behind a tree.

"WaaAHH!" I almost leaped out of my skin with fear. And then I saw that it was that idiot from last night. The one who thought that the sun shone out of his butt.

"Morning, Mr. O.," said Hermie.

"Morning," replied Mr. O. He looked very cool in a fabulous long black leather coat and black baseball cap. *How very* Matrix, I thought as I recalled the outfits in the movie. I had to hand it to Mr. O. that, although clearly out of his mind, he did have a certain sense of style. Not that I was about to let him know that, though. He looked as if he had a big enough ego as it was without me paying him any compliments.

"I . . . I . . . you were there, behind me, all the time? I didn't hear you," I said.

He flashed his grin. "I was playing a part. Don't forget that I am an actor."

"And which part was that, then? A tree?"

Mr. O. looked offended. "Of course not. I was being the invisible man. *I* thought I'd done it rather well."

"But . . . why didn't you let me know that you were there or try to stop me?"

"I had to let you get it out of your system, Leonora. You're a Leo. A fire sign. They never take things lying down, so you were bound to try to escape at least once."

"I wonder why. And why were you following me?"

He pointed at himself and then at me. "Me, guardian, you, Zodiac Girl, remember? What type of guardian do you think I am?"

"Oh, don't start with the Zodiac Girl thing again . . ."

"But I have to. I am here to watch over you. Like the sun over a garden of flowers, ready to bloom."

"Yuck. Pardon me while I puke," I said. "You shouldn't bother. I don't need you."

Hermie took a sharp intake of breath, as if I'd taken it a step too far. He glanced at Mr. O. I noticed that the vein in his forehead was throbbing again. He looked at Hermie.

"Tough girl, isn't she?" he said. "Leo, Leo, lovely Leo." He took a few deep breaths and then turned to me with a cheerful expression that looked fake. "Okay, little brat. Off you go. Go back and get dry while I go and . . . spread a little light around. Yes, that's what I'll do." With that, he turned back off the path and disappeared into the trees, muttering something about having "Never seen anything like her in my life. Spoiled little br . . ."

Seconds later, I was roaring back up the path as the sun rose behind us. *Back to the hotel from hell*, I thought as I clung to Hermie's waist.

Chapter Eight

Breakfast

After Hermie dropped me off, I went straight to the dining room. I sooooo needed some breakfast like I'd never needed breakfast before. Plus, I needed to keep up my strength for later, when the right moment to escape presented itself. My stomach was making strange gurgling nosies because I was so *completely* starving. I'd have even eaten a green apple, if there was one. And that whole-wheat bread, too, if they didn't have croissants. But they were bound to have croissants. Everyone did.

I vaguely remembered where the dining room was from my tour with Mr. O. and soon found the others in there gloomily eating what looked like beige gloop in plastic bowls, while Selene stood behind an enormous pan on a table at the back of the room. She was dressed in a long silver dress and looked like a fairy queen—far out of place in the dismal room where the air smelled like boiled wool. *Ah, happy days*, I thought as I glanced around. *Not.*

"Ew. What is that disgusting stuff?" I asked Jake,

85

who was sitting closest to the door.

"Boiled glue," he said.

"Oatmeal," said Lynn.

"Tastes like glue," said Jake, and he faked his teeth being glued together by it so that he could only chew in slow motion. I almost laughed, but then I remembered that I was very, *very* angry and unhappy.

At that moment, Dr. Cronus came in, and Jake immediately put his bowl on his head, made himself cross-eyed, and started making a noise like a police siren. Oatmeal dripped down his forehead.

I almost laughed again. I could start to like Jake. Poppy would have liked him if she'd been here. One of the best things about her was that she was a giggler and always laughed easily, even when people's jokes weren't that funny. She'd have been on the floor over Jake's antics.

The doctor glanced over at him but didn't even blink an eye.

"Most amusing, boy," he said. "It's not working, though. I know that you're as sane as I am."

"Which isn't very sane," I whispered, "because according to Mr. O., everyone on the staff here thinks that they're planets, so basically, they've all outlooned you."

"Umbongo banana," said Jake, and he leaped up onto the table and went into a monkey impersonation. I hoped that he was still doing his crazy act, because if he wasn't, he was *very* weird.

Dr. Cronus seemed to be counting that we were all present, and then he left the room. I went over to the table where Selene was ladling out the gloop.

"I'll have a chocolate croissant and a hot chocolate," I said.

"Oh, will you? Yes. Well, that *sounds* nice, but we don't have anything like that. This is all there is." And she picked up a ladle full of oatmeal and then let it slop back into the pan with a *splot* sound.

Although the gloop looked disgusting, my stomach was rumbling so much that I decided that I had to give in *just* this once. I had had oatmeal once in a hotel in Scotland, and, if you put enough sugar and fruit on it, it can taste *just* about all right.

"Okay, give me some, but with loads of maple syrup and cream and some peaches."

"I can't do that," she said. She put the lid on the pan and then reached below the counter, found a plastic cup, filled it with water from the sink behind her, and handed it to me.

"What's this?"

"Your breakfast. Tap water."

"Um, excuse me. Reality check. I don't drink tap water. Okay, I did last night, but that was all you gave me. I don't drink just any old brand of water, but *tap* water? And from a plastic cup? I only drink from china and crystal. Now cut out the antics and give me some oatmeal and put it in a DECENT bowl."

"Suit yourself," she said and put the cup back down.

"Isn't there any hot chocolate or cappuccino or something hot?" I asked.

Mark snorted behind me.

"Get a load of 'er," said Marilyn, and she went into a mimic of me. "Ooh, get me an 'ot chocolate, slave. Hey, 'edley-Bent. Sit down and shut up, you posh fool."

"You'll get a mug of tea, if you're lucky," said Lynn.

"I don't want *tea*. I *want* oatmeal," I said through gritted teeth, although a part of me couldn't believe that I was demanding a bowl of what looked like slug slime.

"Say *please*," said Selene. "It's nice to be nice."

I rolled my eyes. "Please," I said wearily. *Honestly*, I thought, *these people, they take life too seriously.*

"No," said Selene.

"*No?* But . . . I just said *please*."

"Mario said no breakfast for talking back to him earlier this morning, and that you have to learn respect. It's in your birth chart. Major lesson to learn. That, and 'Must get in touch with her real feelings and not hold everything in until there's an explosion.' "

"Oh, really? You think that I must learn respect, do you? Get in touch with my feelings? I don't think so. I've seen birth charts. They're all lines and squiggles

88

and angles in a circle. Nothing about respect and no breakfast for naughty Leos. Come on, Moon face, give me a break."

"No. Can't. No oatmeal."

Behind me, Marilyn laughed. I didn't like being laughed at, and she was beginning to annoy me. Before Selene could stop me, I lifted the lid off the oatmeal pan, ladled out a bowl full, and scooped some up into my hand. It felt disgusting, like puréed snail, *and* it was cold, but I didn't care. I turned around and hurled it at Marilyn. It hit her, *splat*, right in the face and began to drip slowly over her forehead.

"I've had enough of you," I said. "You might talk nonsense about being a murderer, and you might scare some wimpy stupid people, but you DON'T scare me."

"Warghhhh, splah . . . wur . . ." Marilyn blustered through the lumpy goo. She wiped a little from her eyes while the rest slid down her cheeks and onto her navy fleece top. "Right, you. You asked for it." She stood up and was about to come toward me.

With the fingers of both my hands, I beckoned her to try it. "Bring it on," I said as I reached in and armed myself with another handful of gunk and looked at Selene. "Hey. You said to get in touch with my feelings, Moon Girl."

"Oh. Oh, dear. I should have known," said Selene. "New moon. At an awkward angle to Mars. People's emotions are always heightened. There was bound to be some kind of fight. Oh. Um . . . come on now, dears. Play nice."

I threw a handful of oatmeal over her, too, and watched with satisfaction as it dripped over her forehead and onto her beautiful silver dress. *So what? What a stupid thing to be wearing in a place like this,* I thought. And anyway, she had been annoying me too, with her hippie manner, ever since the moment I'd first seen her.

"Yeah! Food fight!" yelled Jake, and in a split second he was standing next to me, filling his hands with oatmeal.

Dr. Cronus appeared at the door. "What's all the commotion? I—" *Splot.* Jake hit the old man on his arm with oatmeal and then punched the air with glee. "Result! Excellent." Old Croniepoop dodged out of the way and out the door. Selene followed swiftly behind him.

"Chickens!" I called after them, and then I tucked my hands under my arms and did a little chicken dance. Jake joined in with me.

"Bec, bec, berk, berk, perk," we clucked.

In a flash, the others were at the table, and all of them had handfuls of oatmeal that they were throwing at each other like it was a snowball fight.

For a moment, it almost felt like fun and reminded me of a time when Poppy and I had had a food fight. It was when she was six, and we'd thrown brownie batter around. Even Mom and Dad joined in. That was when we were still a happy family. That was a long time ago.

Splat. Splat. Splot. Oatmeal was being fired everywhere.

And then we heard the door blast open and a very loud whistle.

I stopped mid-hurl and glanced over to see a very angry-looking Mario standing there. He was dressed in a wetsuit, complete with a snorkel *and* flippers, and he was carrying a megaphone. He looked so totally ridiculous that I burst out laughing, but the others stopped what they were doing immediately.

"STEP AWAY from the oatmeal," said Mario through the megaphone. "STEP *AWAY* from the oatmeal."

I couldn't stop laughing, but the others didn't seem to find it as funny.

"Rotten bananas," groaned Lynn. "There goes our hot water for the next week."

"Yeah," snarled Jake, and then he looked in my direction. "And it's all your fault."

Marilyn pointed at me. "Yeah. She started it, sir. She's the troublemaker."

I gave a little curtsy and held up a handful of gloop. "Yeah. Because I AM ZODIAC GIRL, don't you know? A rare honor, I'm told. Anyone like to see what I do as an ENCORE?"

"Out!" commanded Mario. "*All* of you. Assemble in the hall."

Jake, Mark, Lynn, and Marilyn filed out. I stood my ground. I wasn't going anywhere.

"That means you, too, missy."

"Since when do I take orders from you?"

"Since I was told that you were this month's Zodiac Girl and I saw your chart . . ."

I sighed. "Oh, here we go again. I told you—I don't want to be a Zodiac Girl. I can assure you that it's not the honor you think it is. At least not so far . . . Are the others Zodiac Girls and Boys too?"

"Nope. Just you."

"So why me?"

"It's in your stars. You have one month here. Make the most of it. Now MOVE your sorry butt. We're going to hose you all down in the bathroom. With ice-COLD water. That will show you."

"Not me. No way." I decided to show him what I could do if I had a tantrum. I could cause trouble. He would soon see that it would be in his best interest not to get on the wrong side of me. The others might be pussycats, but not this girl. Not *Zodiac Girl*. Ooooh, no. Not me. I roared as loud as I could. Like a lion.

"ReeeeOOOOOOOOOOOOOOAAAAAR!!!"

Mr. O. popped his head around the door when I did that and nodded as if he approved of what he heard. "That's my little Leo. Yes. Yes. Let it all out. Roar like a lion, Leonora. All out. Yes. Good. Fine." And then he disappeared.

I pushed over the oatmeal pan; I kicked the table; I poured water out of all the cups. I hurled a chair at the wall. Roaring all the time. "I DON'T WANT TO BE HERE. YOU CAN'T MAKE ME STAY. I WON'T EAT YOUR OATMEAL. AND I WON'T DO WHAT YOU TELL ME. AND I DON'T WANT TO BE A ZODIAAAAAAAAAAC GIRL."

At one point I glanced over at him to see how upset Mario looked. He wasn't even watching! He was looking out the window as if there was something more interesting going on out there! I. Could. Not. Believe. It. So I picked up the closest bowl and threw it at him, being careful that it went over his shoulder and hit the wall (I didn't want to get him *too* angry), but close enough to make him look. He did duck, but he didn't seem worried.

I threw a few more bowls at the walls, and, being plastic, they bounced off, not that Mario cared. He was looking out the window again. And then he got a newspaper out from somewhere in his wetsuit, sat down, crossed his legs, and began reading it like he was sitting outside a café in the south of France! I looked around to see what else I could trash from the mess in front of me, but I seemed to have thrown just about everything I could.

"Finished?" asked Mario after a while.

I surveyed the destruction in front of me and felt smug. *Good job,* I thought. *That will show him not to mess with me.* "Yeah. I think I might be done. Now. Let that be a lesson to you."

Mario pointed at a closet in the corner of the room. "To me? Oh, no. I don't think so. Dr. Cronus definitely said that the lesson was yours this morning. So. Mops in there. Buckets are in there too. Soap and cleaning products are in the back of the kitchen under the sinks. Now you clean up this mess, and, when the place is sparkling, you can move on."

My stomach suddenly growled a really loud growl, reminding me that I hadn't eaten since yesterday.

"But . . . I . . . I haven't even had any breakfast."

"And who's to blame for that, do you think? Who made this mess? It's in your horoscope that you have to learn that actions have consequences, so you aren't going to get anything to eat until you've cleaned up what you've done in here. You get me?"

"Isn't there anything NICE in my horoscope?"

"Depends on how you play it. What you make of what life gives you."

"Pff. Where's Mr. O.? He's supposed to be my guardian. I'm sure he wouldn't like it if you didn't feed me." I pouted. It was worth a try. I used to be able to wind Daddy around my little finger when I pouted, although that was a long time ago.

"Mr. O. has left the premises for the time being. He isn't too happy with the way you've rejected him, I can tell you that much, so don't be expecting any help from him too soon, not unless you change your attitude, that is. You get me?"

I went to kick a wall.

"Uh-uh . . . I think you get me all right," he said and walked over to the door, where he produced a key. "Now what you probably need is some chill-out time, so I'm going to give you that. Think things over while you're in here. Like it or not, you're going to stay here at this lodge until we say that you can go, and either you play along and make life nice, or you be difficult and make life hard. Your choice. Always will be."

"Bully."

"I'm not a bully. And I'm not the one who had the tantrum here. Now, there's water in the tap there if you get thirsty, and," he said and got up and had a look in the bottom of the pan, "there's just a scrape of oatmeal left too. In the meantime, the sooner you clean up, the sooner you can get out of here."

My answer was to pick up another bowl and throw it at him as he left the room. Once again, it missed and hit the door as it closed behind him, leaving me alone in an oatmeal-covered room.

There was only one thing left to do, and I took a deep breath and let it rip. "Um . . . WAGHHHHHHHHH." I yelled. "WAAAAAAAAAAAAAAAAAAAAAGH!"

I waited. Someone was *bound* to come when they heard that. It was awesome, even by my standards. Someone *always* came running when I really let it rip. But, no. Not even the sound of a footstep creeping to the door to listen to what I was up to, as had happened so often when I'd had a tantrum at my old schools.

I picked up a chair and hurled it against the door. It ricocheted back into the room, since, like the bowls, even the furniture was made of plastic. I made a good commotion, though. *That should bring them running*, I thought.

Nothing.

I tried wailing again. I really did feel angry. But once again—nothing. It was as if they'd forgotten all about me. Or lost interest.

Outside, it was starting to get lighter. I ran to the window and looked out. We were in the middle of nowhere. In front was a landscape of hills and fields, shrubs and trees.

It was my first day. I'd been up barely two hours, and it wasn't even 8:00 yet. How on earth was I going to survive for a whole month here?

Chapter Nine

Routine

I soon got into the routine. *Not* that they had won. I had no choice, not if I was going to survive, and I *am* a survivor. It was play along and be their little Zodiac Girl or starve. Play along or freeze. Play along or be even more miserable than I was on my first night, and I thought at the time that *that* took the prize. But I was wrong. Things got worse, and my time in hell was like this:

5:30 A.M. Wake-up call. Get up. Yeah. 5:30 in the morning!!!!! I used to think that there was only one 5:30 in the day, and that was in the afternoon. Now I knew different. Every morning there was a little note from Mr. O. explaining various aspects of my birth chart and how they were going to appear that day. In other words, outlining what nasty surprises I had in store—there certainly weren't any perks to being a Zodiac Girl, that was for sure.

5:30 – 6:00 A.M. Wash. For the first time in my life, I had to share soap and toothpaste. It was *so* disgusting. The soap smelled like antiseptic. Yuck. I was *sooooo* missing my Goddess products. The most mortifying thing, though, was the first time I washed my hair. There was no conditioner, and then Mario wouldn't let me get my straighteners from my suitcase, which was still locked away.

"Let it dry naturally," he said, thereby revealing just how cruel a torturer he was.

I felt like my world had come to an end. Curly hair. I'd rather die. In the end I had no option but to let it dry on its own, but I pulled it back into a braid before anyone could see how horrible it looked. Then I wore my uniform baseball cap to cover it up further. And mean Selene wouldn't give me any solution for my blue contacts, so I had to go au naturel. Brown eyes. And my nails. I couldn't even look at the sorry sight that they have become after a week of no manicures. There was *no* end to my shame.

6:00 – 7:00 A.M. Breakfast—if you could call it that, but I had to eat *something*. Each night I dreamed about freshly baked croissants and homemade raspberry jam, blueberry muffins, and pastries with hot chocolate. Sadly, dreams don't satisfy your hunger, so I had to eat what there was. Of all the things in this boot camp, having to eat horse food is the second worst (curly hair is the first).

7:00 – 8:00 A.M. Hike around the grounds. Truly. Some days it was raining, one day it even snowed, but that didn't stop old Sergeant Macho Mario from making us march like we were his personal army. And not just march. He made all of us carry heavy backpacks. Every day. In all types of weather. It was completely and utterly and totally the most miserable activity that I had ever done in my entire life. But there was no getting out of it. Not if I wanted to live. Or eat. Or sleep with a pillow.

One day, I pretended to play along with the "planets here as people" idea, and I asked Mario how many planets there were in astrology and how many were here in physical form. "Ten," he replied. I did my math. I'd met only five of them. I figured that the other five might be nicer. Mario said that they could be if you got them on the right day, but they weren't predominant in my chart this month. He has a sneaky answer for everything. I *sooo* hate him.

8:00 – 10:00 A.M. Chores. Yeah. Me, Leonora Hedley-Dent, had to do chores. Cleaning. Peeling potatoes. Polishing furniture. And, actually, it was something to do and made the long days go quicker.

10:00 – 12:00 P.M. Lessons with Dr. Croniebutt. I didn't really know what he was droning on about most days, since I tuned him out. More about the the planets, but I wasn't interested since Mario had told me the other five (Venus, Uranus, Neptune, Pluto, and Jupiter) weren't going to appear like superheroes to make things better. Dr. Cronus could make me sit there, but I didn't have to take it in. All that stuff that Mr. O. had been going on about on the first night, about me being a Zodiac Girl—as far as I was concerned, it was a one-way ticket to Loserville.

12:00 – 1:00 P.M. Lunch. *Lunch!* Ha. Usually soup and a slice of bread. If you were lucky and hadn't had the "privilege" taken away.

1:00 – 4:00 P.M. Gardening. Back outside in the bad weather. Raking leaves. Digging up flower beds. My hands got blisters on them from the shovels, and did anyone care? Not at all.

4:00 – 6:00 P.M. Counseling with Miss Bongo from Bongoland herself, Selene Luna, in the dining room. She had a variety of methods, which entailed dancing around like trees and pretending to be the ocean. I asked her what the point of that was, and she said that it was to get in touch with the free spirit, the nature child that lives within us all. I told her and her nature child to take a running jump off the closest cliff, which made Jake laugh a lot. He seems to think that I am very funny—like a natural comedian. Pff. Just shows what he knows. I was being *deadly* serious.

Another task she got us to do was walk around the room with a partner while one of you closes your eyes and the other one guides. She said it was to encourage working as a team—something that I needed to learn, having seen in my birth chart that I was a double Leo who wanted my own way. *Birth chart, smurf chart*, I thought as I steered Mark into a wall—he got a bloody nose.

Well, serves him right. The silence thing that he does annoys me. Lynn had filled me in on his story. She was good for all the gossip. His dad had lost his job a couple of years ago, and his family was poor, so he started shoplifting so that his family could eat and his younger sister could have presents on birthdays and at Christmas. *Like, boo hoo, not my problem*, I thought.

They were a bunch of losers. All their problems stemmed from being broke, including Marilyn's. Her story was no biggie either. Her dad had left. It was an ugly divorce, and her mom and Marilyn had to move out of their fancy house and live in a smaller place. Worst thing for her, according to Lynn, was not being able to wear her designer clothes anymore, since they couldn't afford it. *Now, that I can relate to*, I thought, as Lynn filled me in on the rest of the story about how Marilyn had become "difficult" and started acting like the tough girl at school. Ha! I could show her difficult at school! I *knew* that murder hadn't even come into it! She was just a classic case of divorce misery, and I'd seen a hundred of those. *Pathetic*, I thought. At my old school, you were the odd one out if your parents were still *together*. In Lynn's case, her dad had died and her mom remarried. She didn't like her stepdad, so she rebelled, and, like me, had been expelled from her last school.

"Sometimes I wish that I'd done it differently," she confessed one night after we'd collapsed into our beds. "I'm not totally stupid, and I can see that, in the end, the person who's suffered most is me. Changing schools meant leaving friends, and now I don't have any. Sometimes I feel lonely. In fact, being in 'ere is the closest I've come to having friends in ages."

"I know what you mean," I said. "I've lost a lot of friends along the way, too. My best friend now is my little dog. Coco."

Lynn smiled. "I've always wanted a pet. My mom always promised I could have one if I behaved. Trouble was, I never did."

Jake's background was the saddest of all. He had a younger brother who was sick, and all the family's money was spent on medical bills. Jake had stolen a car and tried to sell it to raise funds. I *almost* felt sorry for him and the others when their tales of woe came out, but I steeled myself and put up an inner wall just in time. I reminded myself that I didn't let anyone get too close. It only caused pain if I did. I knew that from past experiences. And anyway, I could fix their problems in a second by lending them some cash from my private savings account. I'd ask for interest, of course. It could all be so easily sorted out. I even offered it at a return plus 20 percent, which I thought was very generous, considering the circumstances.

None of them took up the offer, so I pushed down the sympathy that I'd fleetingly felt for them. All their problems could be resolved. Not like mine. None of their stories was as tragic as mine, but they'd never get to hear it, not one of them, not even Lynn.

6:00 – 7:00 P.M. Dinner, which was rice and vegetables or a baked potato and vegetables. Vegetables! *Yeee*-uck. I *so* don't do vegetables. Or at least, didn't used to. I used to think that broccoli was for losers. And now I have to eat it most nights because, if I don't, I don't get anything else. I tried not to think about Tigsy and the stay I missed at the fabulous hotel in Paris. She would have been eating the best of everything. Fashionably tiny meals on divine designer plates, not this plastic garbage they use here. And to *think* of some of the meals that I had sent back because they were too cold or too hot or too slimy! I'd *kill* for them now. Even an avocado would be welcome.

7:00 – 10:00 P.M. Recreation time, meaning more misery in the form of sports activities and workshops, sometimes with Mr. O. and sometimes with Macho Mario. No *real* recreation. Like shopping. Or TV. Or eating chocolate, or anything that reminded me of home. Mr. O. was distinctly cooler with me after the first day when I tried to run away, and he kept muttering under his breath about "a waste of time" and "never in all his days had he met with such ingratitude." *Pfff*, I thought. *He is so used to being the center of attention, which is why he doesn't like it if someone disses him.*

I went along with the routine because I had to, although every day felt like it lasted an eternity. I *even* had to ask permission to go to the bathroom! But there was no escape. I played along, and they thought that I'd given in. Idiots! As if. I hadn't. Not in my head I hadn't. Someone would pay. And when I got out, I'd soon show Mom and Dad how much their little betrayal had *really* cost them!

Of course I did my best to rebel in the first couple of days. Every trick in the book. But these guys were good, they were *very* good, and it was going to take me some time to figure out how to get the better of them. I tried feigning a heart attack, a vomit attack, a headache, a migraine, but they just yawned like they'd seen it all before, and—having witnessed Jake's nut-boy antics and Mark's prolonged silence—I guessed that they had.

In the first week, I went without some meals—like when I discovered I had to actually help cook the food. All I said when asked to chop some onions was "Excuse me, do I look like anyone's slave?" and I wasn't allowed any dinner! My clothes soon began to feel looser because of lack of food.

I went without my pillows as a punishment for running away on my first day, and I went without hot water for starting the oatmeal fight, which was *so* unfair because I did clean up in the end—after around eight hours, in fact, which is something of a record for getting me to do something.

For the first three days, Mario insisted that I was kept away from the others and made me sit in a stone circle in the main hallway. On my own. For hours on end. He told me that he was actually being kind because some inmates had to sit in a stone circle *outside* in the cold, and that's what I'd have to do if I didn't cooperate. And that's when I decided I'd play along for a while. It was sooooooooooooooooooooooo booooooooooooring in that stupid circle, but being thrown out into the freezing December weather would have been even worse. I finally had to give in and say whatever. I decided that I would play the game. Whatever it took to get out of here and back to my normal life.

Some evenings there were more messages from Mr. O. at the foot of my bed. Always about the stars—stuff like, today Mars has been at an angle to Saturn. Or, Pluto was square to the Sun or trident or sextile—with some advice thrown in. I asked the others again about the zodiac thing, and they knew nothing about it. None of them was a Zodiac Girl or Boy, that was for sure. Since they were my only allies in there, I didn't pursue it. I didn't want to be any more of an odd girl out than I already was. I acted like I was going along with it to Mr. O., though, and smiled and thanked him for his kind messages—then I tore them up and put them in the garbage.

One thing I swore to myself was that no one would see me cry. I'd never let them know that they had upset me. And one of these days, I would get my revenge. And *then* they'd be sorry.

One of the weekly tasks in counseling was to write a letter home. My first one went like this:

GET ME OUT *OF HERE!!! NOW!!!!!*

But then Loony Pants Selene took a look at it and told me that I had to do it again. "Dig deep, my little flower," she said. "Tell them how you really feel."

So I wrote this:

Mom and Dad, (I wrote Dear Mom and Dad and then realized that they *weren't* dear, not to me. Not anymore. So I crossed out the "Dear.") *GET ME OUT OF HERE NOW!!!! I HATE YOU. I am locked up with a bunch of crazy people who think that they are planets!!!*

That letter got vetoed as well.

"You asked me to dig deep, and I did," I said. "That's how I feel."

Loony made me do a third one:

Mr. and Mrs. Hedley-Dent,

I have been instructed that I have to write you a letter as a weekly task. I do this under pressure, like everything else in this cold, miserable, godforsaken place, because I have learned that if I don't do what I am told, then I am punished or starved. I HATE you more than ever and can't believe that you have made me suffer in this way. When I get out of this prison sentence you have put me through, I will be going to live with someone else. I disown you as my parents. And I will sell my story to the papers so that everyone knows what horrible people you are. And then you'll be sorry. So there.

Take care of Coco.

From Leonora Hedley-Dent

"I am soooo going to make my parents pay for this," I said to Lynn at the end of week one as we went to the gym for our sports activities.

"Yeah," she said. "In the meantime, though, I wonder what torture Mario has lined up for us this evening."

We didn't have to wait long to find out. Mr. O. came jogging around the corner. He looked ridiculous. He was dressed in a white sweatsuit with what looked like a white cashmere scarf tossed casually around his neck. His sneakers were pure white too, like they'd never been worn outside. With his dazzling good looks, he always looked like he was about to go into a photo shoot for a men's magazine—not a hair out of place, his teeth brighter than white, his skin so tanned that it was almost orange.

"Hedley-Dent, you're with me," he said. "The rest of you, Mario said meet him out front for a night hike."

"Oh, nooooooooo," groaned Jake. "Not again."

"Fresh air is good for the soul," said Mr. O., who then indicated that I should follow him. I slouched along behind him as he led me into the gym and flicked on the lights. Hanging from the ceiling was what looked like an enormous sausage.

"What is *that*?" I asked.

Mr. O. flashed his bright smile. "*That* is whatever you want it to be."

"Ah. So it's a private plane to get me out of here?"

"No need to be sarcastic, Leonora. Didn't you get my zodiac message this morning?"

I shrugged. "Yeah." Like all the messages, I had cast a cursory glance over it before putting it in the garbage. It had said something about the Moon being square to Mars.

"Emotions that are hard to express can manifest in anger or impatience, especially for a Leo. I'm going to show you another way to get them out."

"Whatever," I said and pointed back at the sausage thing. "So. What is it?"

"It's a punching bag."

"You're going to teach me how to box?"

109

"Not exactly."

"So what, then?"

"Go and give it a punch, and you'll see," he said. "I'll show you how."

He pranced off toward the bag and starting taking jabs at it in the way that you see boxers doing when they're in training for a fight. After a few minutes he stopped, went to the equipment closet at the back of the gym, pulled out a pair of boxing gloves, and tossed them to me. "Your turn."

I put on the gloves, approached the bag, and gave it a tap.

"Put some *elbow* into it, girl," commanded Mr. Razzle-Dazzle.

I gave it another tap.

"Nooooo, like this," said Mr. O., as he ran toward the bag and whacked it. "Come on, Leonora. *Go* for it."

I gave it a few more halfhearted taps. Like, boxing is *so* last decade. "Okay. Okay. I'm doing it. I'm doing it."

Mr. O. started prancing around me, making little jabbing, punching motions. "Hit it, go on. Hit it."

He was starting to annoy me. I hit the bag with a little more force.

"*That's* more like it. Come on. Let's get a little energy up here. Come *ON*. Show me what you're made of."

I stopped and yawned. "I am *so* not interested in this.

Like, give me a break. You're supposed to be my guardian, aren't you? Don't I get some time off for good behavior? Time off for being a Zodiac Girl or whatever?"

"This *is* your time off. You could be out there hiking with the others."

"Ooh. Excuse me if I don't fall over with gratitude."

"Excused," said Mr. O., flashing me a grin.

"I was being sarcastic."

"So was I."

He started ducking and diving around me, pretending that I was the punching bag, although he didn't touch me. Jab, jab. It was getting very, *very* annoying. "Go on, punch the bag, *punch* the bag."

So I did. I *really* punched it.

Mr. O. continued dancing behind me. "Excellent. Now. Who makes you mad?"

"You do."

"Then pretend the bag is me."

I did. And I whacked the bag with all my might.

Jab, jab. Mr. O. continued around my head like he was a fly, buzzing around. Jab, jab, buzz, buzz. "Now, who else annoys you?"

"*All* of you here."

"Great. Good. Now pretend the bag is Dr. Cronus."

I whacked it. "Take that old Wiz Woz."

"*Wiz Woz?*"

"Yeah. Cronus looks like an old wizard."

"I guess he does. Now, do Selene," said Mr. O., all the while continuing to dance around me in a circle, jabbing the air with his clenched fists.

I whacked the bag again. "And you, Miss Hippie Happy Clappy."

Mr. O. snorted with laughter. "*Hippie Happy Clappy.* Ha! And your mom and dad. You're mad at them, aren't you?"

He was talking fast and spinning around me in circles, and when he mentioned Mom and Dad, I felt the rage that I'd been holding back all week while I'd been doing my Miss Play-Along role rise up to the surface. I began to hit the bag. *Whack. Whack. Thwack.*

Mr. O. was gleeful and punched the air. "Who else? Who else?"

"Henry. *Grrrrrr.*" Mr. O. didn't have to encourage me this time. I'd gotten the hang of it, and, once I'd started, I couldn't stop. It was like a tsunami of rage was flooding through me, and I was helpless to stop it. "WAAAAAAAAAAAAAGHHH!"

I whacked Henry with all I had. Then Shirla for not coming with me on the plane. And Mr. Nash at my last school for expelling me. And Mrs. Simons. And Principal Ericson. And Polly James in my last dorm. And . . . there was a long list of contenders lining up in my head to have their faces imprinted on the punching bag. I went for it. Punch. *Thwack.* Punch.

Thwack. And a few kicks for good measure. *Thwackawackawacka-wackawack*. I whacked away until there was no more whack left inside of me. I was whacked out. I bent over to catch my breath. I was red in the face. And perspiring. And then *she* was there, a face at the end of the line of people to be angry at. I took a sharp intake of breath and pushed her back into the recesses of my mind. But she'd been there for a second. Mo Bolton. Looming up like an ominous shadow with that snide look that she'd always had when she sensed a fight was about to happen.

Mr. O. seemed to sense that I'd reached some type of wall or door inside of myself. "Enough?"

I held up a hand. "Enough."

"Take a few breaths, Leonora," said Mr. O., and then he added gently, "You did well. You did really well."

And the strange thing was, I *felt* good, just for a few seconds. Like I'd released something from deep inside of me.

And then suddenly I felt very tired. I crumpled to the floor and lay with my arms out like a cross. Mo must not be allowed out. I must not even think of her. What she did. And even worse, what she made *me* do to Poppy.

Chapter Ten

Bah humbug!

It was December 24th–Christmas Eve–and just after breakfast. I'd been at the funny farm for almost three miserable, stinking weeks. Mr. O. had left his usual note this morning, something about Saturn and Pluto and restrictions. I don't know why he bothered. The messages didn't make any sense. Plus, there had been something about Mars moving into Aquarius, which would bring about a more relaxed feeling, with Jupiter putting in an appearance. *Like, what on Earth is he talking about?* I thought. *Relaxed about being here for Christmas? Is that supposed to make me feel better?* I was counting down the days. Counting down the hours. Counting down the minutes until I could get out of there and back to my life.

We'd just finished eating our bowls of gloop, and I'd been trying not to imagine what I would have been eating for breakfast if I was at home (fresh almond pastries flown in from a little patisserie in Belgium, fresh raspberries with fresh cream, and hot chocolate), when Mario appeared with boxes of Christmas decorations.

He spilled tinsel, red and gold stars, and ornaments out onto the table. "Mark, Jake, you two go out into the grounds and cut holly and ivy. Girls, you make a start in the hall."

I'd behaved myself for three weeks, and today I wasn't in the mood. I picked up the last spoon of oatmeal and turned it over so that it fell back into my bowl with a splat. "Duh. Why?" I asked without looking up.

"To make it festive," he said.

"Do it yourself," I said, putting down my spoon and crossing my arms. "Like, what did your last slave die of?"

"*What did your last slave die of?*" Mario mimicked. "Not that routine again. Come on, Hedley-Dent, if you're going to insult me, for heaven's sake, come up with something new. In the meantime, decorations, Christmas, the season to be jolly. Let's do it."

"The others can, but count me out."

"It's a team task," said Mario. "We'll all help out."

"Not me."

"And, may I ask, why not?"

"I don't do Christmas."

Mark, Jake, Lynn, and Marilyn were all watching the exchange as if it was a tennis match.

"Ah," said Mario. "You might not, but we do."

"Listen, soldier boy," I said, "you might not have

noticed, but I have been brought here against my will. I have been separated from my parents. And so far I have played along. Hiked when you said hike. Cleaned when you said clean. Jumped when you said jump. But decorate this dump? Forget it. As I said, I *don't* do Christmas. End of story."

Mario narrowed his eyes. "You either cooperate or take time out on your own to think things over."

"So what? You can't make me."

"I . . . think . . . it would be . . . in your best interest to help with the decorations."

"And *I* say bah *HUMBUG*. What part of that do you *not* understand?"

"*What* is your problem, Hedley-Dent? Would you like to share it with the group?"

"Yeah. Sure. Mark, Jake, Lynn, Marilyn, I hate Christmas and everything that goes with it. I can't wait for it to be over. Okay, I've shared. Happy now?"

"Okay. Fair enough, but you have had it explained to you a thousand times," Mario droned on. "Three weeks you've been here, and you still haven't got it. As with all exercises that are done as a team, your behavior affects everyone else."

"What? So we all have to go and sit in your stupid stone circle?"

"No. Only you. But I'm giving you until five o'clock exactly. If you aren't ready to join in by then, your bad mood will affect the whole group."

"Yeah, like they care for one second what's happening with me."

"Oh, I think that they will today," said Mario, "because if you don't come and join in, no dinner. For *anyone*."

"That's not fair, sir," said Jake.

Mario turned to Jake and fixed him with a stare. "Did I give you permission to speak?"

"No, sir."

"Then be quiet. You were saying, Hedley-Dent?"

"Oooooh, no dinner, sir. Like there's anything to miss. A bit of moldy old potatoes and carrots. They'll probably thank me."

"Ah, no. Tonight is special. It's Christmas Eve, and a friend of ours is bringing us a feast from the local deli."

"Yeah, right," I scoffed. "It's all part of the torture. You're teasing us."

"No. Didn't you read your horoscope this morning? About Jupiter?"

Lynn suddenly pointed out the window. "Oh, my God," she interrupted. "No. He's telling the truth. Look what's being unloaded out at the back."

Jake, Mark, and Marilyn got up and went to join her at the window. Jake punched the air. "Yesss! Get a load of that grub coming in!"

I waited for a few moments, but then I got up and sauntered over to the window. But I did it in a really casual way, to show that I didn't really care.

Outside, the sky was dark with heavy black clouds, but, sure enough, by the kitchen door was a big white van with the back doors wide open and a light on. A big, jolly-looking man was busy unloading boxes and platters. He had dark hair, but, in the right wig and beard, he was the type of person who would have made an excellent Santa Claus.

"Come on, let's go to the kitchen," said Lynn, and then she glanced back at Mario. "Oh, yeah. I mean . . . permission to go, sir?"

"Granted," said Mario.

Mark, Jake, Marilyn, and Lynn sped off. Mario looked at me and raised an eyebrow as if to say, are you going to go too?

"Well, I might as well," I said as I got up to go with the others. "Anything's better than staying in here with you."

The first thing that hit me when I opened the kitchen door was the warmth coming from a roaring fire in the fireplace and a yummy smell of cinnamon and oranges coming from a pan on the stove. The room had been transformed and felt delightfully festive. There was even music, carols playing out of hidden speakers. But, best of all, the long table was packed with food fit for a banquet.

The jolly-looking man came in, put down an enormous platter of the most delicious-looking cookies, and pointed at the stove. "I made some apple cider," he said. "My own special recipe. You all look like you could use a little cheering up. Nonalcoholic, of course. Help yourselves."

"Meet Joe," said Mario, coming in behind me. "He runs a deli in a village not too far from here. Best chef in the land—in the world, in fact."

Joe nodded and beamed. "In the universe! *And* I'm the manifestation of Jupiter. Jupiter being the planet of expansion and jollity."

Lynn and Marilyn exchanged glances. "Head case," said Lynn under her breath.

"Who cares?" commented Marilyn. "As long as we get some of that food."

"So, where's the Zodiac Girl?" asked Joe.

"*Zodiac Girl?* What *is* this stuff about zodiacs?" asked Jake as he looked around. "Leonora mentioned it the other day. What's going on?"

I could see that Joe was about to come out with some nonsense similar to that which Mr. O. came out with, and I didn't want him drawing attention to me with any crazy ramblings. I'd learned long ago that, if you're singled out as odd, you get picked on.

"I think it's some type of club they're all in, like a zodiac club. Best to play along with these crazy people,

119

especially if we're going to get the food," I whispered to Jake, Mark, Marilyn, and Lynn. Then I turned to Joe. "Yeah, yeah, me, them, we're all zodiac people here. Hello, Jupiter. Welcome to the lodge. The food looks good. Need a hand bringing it in?"

Joe raised an eyebrow and exchanged looks with Mario.

"She's a tough one," said Mario. "A double Leo."

"Ah," said Joe, and he rubbed his hands and gave me a wink. "Okay, guys. Help yourselves to apple cider."

Jake was over by the pan in a flash, ladling out five cups of the hot amber liquid, which he handed around. I took my first sip and had to hold back from gasping with delight. It was the most divine drink I had ever tasted, spicy and sweet at the same time. If the food was as good as this, we were in for a real treat.

We drank the first cup, and then Jake refilled our glasses, and all the while Joe brought in more and more food. I thought that I'd never seen anything more beautiful. An enormous turkey. Platters of sausages wrapped in bacon. Mini pizzas. Roast potatoes. Pastries and cakes of every type—frosted and fruit, some with marzipan. Chocolate mousse. Pecan pie. Huge bunches of grapes. White and red. Strawberries. Raspberries. A platter of cheeses. Tubs of ice cream: caramel pecan, pistachio, mocha fudge, chocolate chip. Bottles labeled: maple syrup, hot fudge, caramel. And trays of candy: jelly beans, chocolate-covered raisins, marshmallows, and chocolates of every shape and size.

My mouth began to water, and I could see that the others were feeling the same. Mark was almost drooling.

"Thank you, God or Jupiter or Santa or whoever's up there!" cried Jake and pointed to what looked like an apple pie. "Get a load of that big pie. *Yeee*-um."

"So," said Mario, coming up behind to join us, "Leonora, do you think that now you might join us in the team task of decorating?"

He must think that I am such a pushover, I thought, as I dragged my eyes away from a triple-layer vanilla cake that oozed sugary goodness.

"This is bribery," I said. "And it will all go in my story to the press."

"Oh, knock it off," growled Marilyn. "Stop acting like the brat princess. We're all starving and know that you are too. And you don't need to worry about being fat anymore, 'cause you've gotten thinner in the past fcw weeks."

People making comments about whether I was fat or thin always made me angry. Seeing all the food made me angry. The way that everyone was acting so desperate made me angry. Angry. Angry. *Angry*. In my previous life I could have snapped my fingers, and a similar feast would have arrived in a flash. Okay. So I hadn't eaten much for a few weeks, but I wasn't going to crack that easily!

"No. You knock it off. And if *you* call me *brat princess* once more," I said as I took a step toward her and squared up to her, "I'll show you *just* how bratty and how princessy I can be!"

"Now then, girls," warned Mario.

But Marilyn and I weren't listening. We stood across from each other.

"Oh, God," said Lynn. "Eye fight. Eye fight."

"Don't do it, Marilyn," Jake pleaded. "She could really ruin things."

"Yeah," begged Lynn. "Just leave it."

But Marilyn's eyes didn't leave mine.

And my eyes didn't leave hers.

Our eyes were locked. Single combat. No weapons required.

This I can do, I thought as I stared back at her. Never mind calling me a princess, when it comes to staring down an opponent, I was the queen—champion at all my previous schools. I could make my eyes go out of focus so that the person I was looking at went blurry. They couldn't tell by looking at me, but it meant that I didn't get intimidated by the other person's stare. It had worked every time, aside from with Mario, but he was in a league of his own.

Seconds went by . . .

Minutes . . .

The only sound was the fire crackling in the fireplace. And seven people breathing.

Then, finally, Marilyn blinked.

"*Brrrrat* . . . pr . . . in . . . cess," she said *very* slowly, almost spitting her words.

I nodded smugly. "Your choice." I turned to Mario.

"Noooooooooo!" cried Jake and Lynn in unison. "Please, Leonora, think of all that lovely food. Please."

"Noooooooooooooooooooooooo!" cried Marilyn. "Please, Leonora, don't mess it up for the rest of us. Please. I didn't mean it."

"Too late," I said.

"N . . . n . . . nooooooooooooooooooo!" cried Mark, and all eyes turned to him in amazement.

"You *spoke*!" Jake exclaimed.

I wasn't moved. It took more than some roast potatoes and a vanilla cake to break me. "Stone circle, please, Mario. And you can tell that fat deli man he may as well put the dinner back in the van."

I heard a collective gasp and a sob from Jake.

Mario nodded. "Follow me," he said. "You have until five o'clock to change your mind. And bear in mind that you will not only be ruining Christmas Eve for yourself, but also for your fellow guests." He shook his head sadly. "You just don't get being a team player, do you? It's still me, me, me in your world. Where does it get you, huh?"

"Suits me," I said, and I pointed at Marilyn. "*She* asked for it."

I took one last look at the feast and then walked out, following Mario like a condemned prisoner going to the gallows.

Marilyn, Mark, Jake, and Lynn stood to one side, their heads bowed.

"Brat princess walking," said Jake as I went past him. "Stand back. Let her through."

Chapter Eleven

Christmas past

I sat in my stone circle in the hallway. I stared at the wood-paneled walls. I stared at the high ceiling. The paint up there was dingy with age. There was a cobweb in one corner. The only sounds were the ticking of the antique clock on the wall and the occasional gust of wind outside that rattled the windows and doors.

It was boring being there. And it was lonely.

But I wasn't giving in for anybody.

I took a nap. I rearranged the stones. I rearranged the stones again. *So much for Mars moving into Aquarius and life getting more relaxing*, I thought. *It's so relaxing that I feel comatose.*

During the afternoon, Mark, Jake, Lynn, and Marilyn crept into the hall, one after another, and tried to reason with me.

Lynn offered to give me her pillow on nights when I'd lost the privilege of mine.

Jake offered to help with my chores.

Even Mark came and, having recovered his voice, had a lot to say: "Please, Leonora, don't ruin it for the others. It's bad enough being in this miserable place on a night like this. Let's at least have a decent dinner. And, speaking for myself, I've never seen a feast like the one in the kitchen. And neither have the others. You've known what it's like to have the best. None of us have."

I shook my head. I couldn't back down and lose face. Not at this stage of the game.

Marilyn came and threatened me. "If you don't come out of this circle this minute and 'elp us decorate, I will cut off your arm with my penknife and beat you with the soggy end."

"Oh, *très amusant*, Marilyn. Is that all?" I said, and then I yawned and turned away from her. "Be quiet when you go, okay? I think I might take a little nap."

Cut off my arm with her penknife. She was so pathetic. I also suspected that she put on the tough accent. She didn't need to threaten me or worry. None of them should. I was sure that they would get their special dinner. They hadn't done anything wrong. It was me who was going to be excluded. A special treat for Zodiac Girl. Mario and his crew wouldn't deny the others because I was being stubborn. Not on Christmas Eve. No one would be that mean.

I lay down on the floor and curled up like a cat to try to stay warm, since there was a serious draft blasting in from under the front door, and there I fell into a fitful sleep. I was awoken by four chimes from the clock down the hall. It was dark and cold, and I felt cramped and uncomfortable.

For a moment I wished that Mr. O. had been around a little more. Okay, so he was a bit of a kiss-kiss actor type, but he was a lot more fun than the others, and although I would never let him know it, not in a million squillion years, I recognized a kindred spirit in him. He was clearly used to being the star of the show, just like I was, which is probably why he took it so personally when I was rude to him.

As I lay there, I wondered what might have happened if I hadn't stomped on my zodiac phone and had taken more of an interest in his obscure little notes. Maybe they were coded with clues about how to get out of here. He had said that he was my guardian, so maybe he had been trying to help me in some peculiar way. *Maybe I've been playing it all wrong*, I wondered. *Didn't Mr. O. say something about what you resist persists? Maybe I shouldn't have resisted being a Zodiac Girl or a team player. Maybe I should have welcomed it and seen where it could have led.*

I sat up and rubbed my arms to try to get warm again, and a couple of seconds later Dr. Cronus appeared.

"And have you learned your lesson?" he asked.

"Only thing I've learned is that this floor certainly is hard. So can I get up now?"

He nodded. I took that as a sign that I could go and

have dinner. I couldn't wait. I was starving. I'd been dreaming about all the gorgeous food that had appeared earlier in the day, so I raced to the kitchen, where I expected to find the others munching away. I prayed that they'd saved a piece of something for me.

However, the scene in the kitchen had changed since this morning. The fire had gone out. The only smell in the air was the usual one of boiled onions and bleach. And there were no more Christmas carols playing. Four teenagers sat slumped at the table under a glaring overhead light. In front of them was a large pan.

"What's that?" I asked.

"Potato soup," growled Lynn.

"*Potato soup!* But . . . but where's all the yummy food?"

Four faces turned to look accusingly at me.

"They took it back, thanks to you," said Marilyn through clenched teeth.

"No!" I gasped.

"And we had to eat this disgusting stuff that tastes like puréed flour," Jake added. "All because of you."

"You're the most selfish person we have ever met," said Mark.

"And we all *hate* you," said Lynn.

A wave of disappointment flooded through me. No Christmas dinner. Not a morsel. Not a crumb. I was going to fade away completely if this continued. Forget size zero. I was going to be size *minus* zero.

Vibrations of loathing were flying through the air toward me, so real that I could almost see them, like snakes writhing toward me, with tiny tongues poking venom in my direction. For the second time in my life, I, Queen of I Can Stare You Back, couldn't meet someone's angry gaze. I looked away and then ran to the dorm, where I flung myself on my narrow bed and pulled the blanket over my head.

It wasn't *fair*. Okay. Maybe I should've said I was sorry to them, but I didn't think that they'd really be punished for my behavior. Not really. *Nobody understands*, I thought as I brought the back of my right hand up to my forehead like a tragic heroine. *No one can ever understand.*

"Leonora, Le . . . o . . .NoR . . . a . . ." called a soft voice.

I poked my head out of the blanket to see that Dr. Cronus was standing in the doorway. He looked weird. Shimmery. I looked closer and realized that he was holding a flashlight under his chin, which made him look like a ghost. Poppy and I used to do that to scare each other under the blankets on Halloween, and then we'd tell ghost stories.

Ha! I thought. *New tactic. So now they're going to try to scare me into submission.* "Cut the bogeyman act, Doc. I'm not falling for it."

Dr. Cronus sighed and then turned off the flashlight. "Worth a try," he said. He beckoned me to follow him out the door.

"Why out the door?" I asked. "Why not fly right out the window like Peter Pan and Wendy, huh? Come on, Crustyboots. Show me what you've got."

Dr. Cronus sighed again. "I do *so* hate you spoiled brats. I always get assigned to you. It's because I'm the Great Taskmaster, you know. He who teaches life's important lessons—and it does get oh, so tiresome sometimes when people resist, which they always do at the beginning. Some days I wish I could be one of the others. Like Joe. He's Jupiter, you know. Everybody loves him. Or Hermie. He's my grandson and very popular."

"Oh, drop the poor-me act. If you don't like what you're doing, get lost. I never asked you to teach me lessons or whatever."

"I have no choice," said the doctor. "You are Zodiac Girl, so I can't get lost, no matter how much I want to. You have been chosen, and I must do what I have been bidden. So get up."

"Or else?"

Mr. O. suddenly appeared behind him. "Or else the others won't get their Christmas breakfast or dinner either," he said.

"Christmas breakfast? There's going to be a Christmas *breakfast*? And a Christmas dinner?"

"Well, that all depends on you, Leonora," said Mr. O. "You have been one of the most resistant Zodiac Girls we have ever had, and now enough's enough. It was up to you what you did with your month here, and so far, quite frankly, it's been a waste of everyone's time. But it doesn't need to be if you'll just let us in a little. You have so much going for you if you would just let down the wall you've put up to push the world away. Okay, so, yes, Leos want their own way, and yes, they can be stubborn. But they can also be strong and generous and affectionate and the best fun. Why not be the best you can be instead of always choosing to be the worst?"

I was about to say something snide back, but there was some truth in what Mr. O. had said. I knew that I was demanding, and I did always push people away, and where had it gotten me? This miserable lodge on Christmas Eve, and everyone here hated me.

"Let us help you," said Mr. O., "and your time here doesn't need to be so bad."

I nodded. "Okay. Lead the way," I said with a sigh. Mr. O. smiled at me and then left me alone with the doctor, who beckoned me to follow him out of the dorm and down through the maze of corridors until we got to a staircase at the back of the lodge. It led down to another floor that I hadn't noticed before.

"What's down there?" I asked.

"Come with me, and you'll see."

The staircase had a dark wooden banister and went down one flight to a door that was carved with intricate figures. On closer inspection, I could make out the 12 signs of the zodiac.

"A zodiac door," I said as I read the words under the carvings. "Aries the ram, Taurus the bull, Gemini the twins, Cancer the crab, Leo the lion—that's me—Virgo the virgin, Libra the scales, Scorpio the scorpion, Sagittarius the archer, Capricorn the goat, Aquarius the water bearer, and Pisces the fish. Hey, this is really beautiful. Is it Indian? It looks Eastern."

Dr. Cronus smiled. "It's from Atlantis. The only one like it in existence."

"Cool. Atlantis. Yeah. I think I know someone who went there on vacation."

Dr. Cronus almost laughed. "I very much doubt that. Atlantis is an ancient civilization."

"Yeah, so? Greece and Italy are ancient too. I'm not totally stupid. People go there on vacation."

Dr. Cronus tutted. "I sincerely doubt that they have been to Atlantis," he said. "Not unless they can time-travel." He got out a huge brass key and opened the door. "You're very chatty all of a sudden."

"Just glad to be out of that stone circle," I said. "It was very boring."

Dr. Cronus turned on a light, and a room with floor-to-ceiling bookshelves appeared. They were weighed down with ancient-looking books, videos, and DVDs. I looked at a couple of the labels. *Polarities and Elements*.

Hmm. *That sounds complicated,* I thought. *The Quadrupicities.* Ditto. *Progressions. Transits. Synastry in Action.*

"Hey, this is like the type of library a wizard would have. In fact, you look like a wizard."

Dr. Cronus sighed. "If I had a penny for every time I've heard that. Just because I have a long white beard, it doesn't make me a wizard. And anyhow, our aim is to teach you to see the magic that there already is in the world. Not to do tricks."

"Yeah, yeah. Whatever," I said, and then I remembered what Mr. O. had just said and smiled at Dr. Cronus to show that I wasn't totally against him. "Hey, got any magazines down here? Like *Teen Vogue* or *Elle*?"

Dr. Cronus turned and gave me a scathing look.

"I'll take that as a 'no,' then. But what is this place?"

"My archive, and I suggest that you go and sit down and be quiet while I find your file," said Dr. Cronus. He pointed at a TV screen at the end of the room, in front of which was an old leather couch with some of its stuffing coming out. "Go and sit down there and wait for me."

I did as I was told and made myself comfortable on the couch. On the table in front of me there were two sandwiches and a glass of milk.

"That's for you!" he called. "Avocado and cheese."

"Hey, thanks, Doc," I said and gulped the first one down in about four bites. It was utterly yummy.

"And don't call me 'Doc.' I'm Dr. Cronus to you. Ah,

there it is," I heard him say, and, moments later, he appeared with what looked like a DVD in his hand. He put it into the machine.

"Movie?" I asked. "We're going to watch a *movie?*"

The doctor nodded. "We use all the latest technology when we can. Now, as you know, I am also known as Saturn . . ."

"The taskmaster," I said, to show that I had listened to *some* of what he and Mr. O. had been droning on about.

Dr. Cronus nodded. "Saturn rules the part of one's life in which one needs to learn lessons. In your case, in order to do this, we need to go back into your past and look at some of the fears that lie there."

I felt a shiver of panic. My past? He was beginning to scare me, but . . . he couldn't know about my past. *Could he?* I wondered as I began to eat my second sandwich.

"Don't be scared, Leonora," said the doctor. "You can overcome your past. Your chart shows many strengths as yet untapped. Now watch the screen."

The blank screen grew light. A door appeared. A green door with a brass lion's head on it. It looked familiar. The door began to open. It *was* familiar.

A lump came into my throat, and I stopped mid-munch.

"How . . . ?" I began, but no more words came as I continued to watch. It was our old house on the TV. Our house in England where we lived before Poppy died.

From the back of the house came the sound of laughter, and the camera zoomed in. I felt like I was there. Walking down the hall like I had a hundred times when I'd lived there. The door to the living room opened, and I felt as if someone had punched me in the stomach, because there was Poppy, her face lit up with laughter.

"How? *Where* did you get this?" I asked. I had never seen it before. I knew that there were videos and DVDs of Poppy, but I thought that I had seen them all. Knew each one frame by frame. I'd memorized every second of each one of them because they were all that I had left of her.

Dr. Cronus sat on a chair to my left and put a finger up to his lips to indicate that I should be quiet. "Just watch."

Poppy was sitting by the fire and cutting out patterns from a piece of green paper in front of her.

"Leaves," I said. "She's making leaves for decorations."

For a few seconds my questions fell away. I didn't care how Dr. Cronus had gotten the DVD or why. I could see Poppy. My little sister at Christmas.

She was two years younger than me, had blond hair and was pretty in a delicate way, with eyes that were almost too big for her face, giving her a look of constant surprise at the world. She was never completely healthy and was thin and pale as far back as I could remember. She suffered from asthma attacks that would come on out of the blue and were frightening to witness as she struggled to breathe with the aid of her inhaler. She had the horrible thing near her on the table. I couldn't help but notice it.

Not that she ever complained, I thought as I watched the screen. *She was always positive and generous to a fault. She'd always get anything I wanted just so that she could be with me. And she loved to play beauty salon and would brush my hair for ages and not complain if I squirmed my way out of returning the favor. I did love her. I did. In my own way. If I had known what was going to happen, of course I would have let her know just how much a lot more often.*

"What are you thinking about, Leonora?" asked Dr. Cronus as the image of her lingered for a moment. Then the screen went blank.

"Nothing," I replied as I played with the locket around my neck. "Just plotting my revenge on my parents and how I'm going to get the press to come here and close this place down for cruelty to children."

"Is that right?" asked Dr. Cronus. He looked disappointed. "Fine. You do that, then. First of all, though, I have a task for you."

"Okay, no, not more dishes to do . . ."

"Come with me," said Dr. Cronus, and he went over and pushed on one of the bookshelves. It opened up to what looked like a secret room behind.

"Cool," I said. "A secret door. Is it a way out?"

"Yes and no," said the doctor as he beckoned me to go through. "It could be a way out for you if you complete the task."

I sighed. "How did I know that you were going to say something like that?"

I went into the small room. It had no window and was more like a large closet. On the right side was an enormous pile of toys. They were of every variety: dolls, robots, stuffed animals, cars, planes, trains, games. Next to the toys were boxes that, on closer inspection, contained bath sets, books, CDs, DVDs, handkerchiefs, scarves, gloves, perfumes . . .

"What is this?" I asked. "A collection for a garage sale?"

"Certainly not," huffed Dr. Cronus. "It's all brand-new. And it's your next task. Not cleaning up. Wrapping up."

"*Wrapping up?*"

Dr. Cronus nodded and pointed to a table on the left of the room where there were rolls and rolls of wrapping paper, ribbons, strings of tinsel, scissors, glue, and tape. "You can come out when you're finished," he said. "These are gifts for people who are going to be in the local hospital over Christmas. Old and young. It is time for you to take some sort of positive action. You must do this if you are going to overcome your past and move forward."

"Do something positive?"

"You heard me."

I looked at the mounds of presents. "*All* of them? You expect me to wrap *all* of them?"

"All of them. Leos can be very creative if they want to be, fabulously flamboyant, in fact. It's time you got back in touch with the more giving side of your nature. And think over things while you're at it. I'm going to leave you now. There's some juice in a carton behind the door and a buzzer to the right of it. You can press it when you're finished." He gave me a totally false smile and then left the room and shut the door behind him.

I got up and tried the door. Locked. I glanced around the room. There was definitely no escape.

I sat on the floor and stared at the pile of presents for a few minutes. *I could break them,* I thought. *Rip off the dolls' heads, pull off their arms, and wrap them around the teddy bear's neck. I could empty all of the bath gel over the walls. Stomp on the toy trains and cars until they're nothing but splinters. Break everything! That would show old Cronie Baby what he can do with his precious lessons.* I considered the plan for a few moments. The old me would have started in an instant and created havoc, but I found myself hesitating. There was no point. I knew my captors well enough by now to know that if I didn't cooperate, they'd only find some other miserable task for me to do. And it was pointless having a tantrum, since they'd pay no attention or leave me in here for even longer.

I took a deep breath and picked up the first present. *I may as well get started,* I thought. *Just do the job and get it over with. The sooner it's done, the sooner I can get out of here.*

I began wrapping, using the most basic wrapping paper, and continued doing each present as fast as I could with no fancy trimmings. As I worked, my mind drifted back to Christmases gone by when Poppy had been alive and she and I would sit together and wrap all the presents. She delighted in every aspect of Christmas—making handmade cards with glitter and stars, decorating the tree with gingerbread men, leaving out milk and cookies for Santa and apples for his reindeer, and then opening her presents on the morning of December 25th. Her enthusiasm had been infectious, and I had loved the season and all that went with it—the carol services, the shopping, the yummy dinner with family and friends.

As I continued wrapping, I remembered how I loved to buy presents for everyone and then wrap them in my own special way. Mommy said I had a gift for wrapping—an artist's touch. My presents always looked the best and hardly cost anything. It didn't take much. I liked to use what I could find in the garden. In December there was always holly and ivy to pick. I used to weave the green leaves and red berries with pieces of twigs that I'd spray gold and then put it all together with green ribbon. I was such a different person back then. I'd even write my own plays about princes and princesses and fairies in faraway lands.

Poppy used to watch me perform them with her enormous brown eyes, and I'd feel like I was making magic in front of her.

And now I'm here in a closet on my own on Christmas Eve, and everybody hates me. And I am so-ooooo sa-aaaaadddddddd. Probably the loneliest person in the whole world. A tidal wave of self-pity flooded through me. Tears came to my eyes. *Poor, poor me. All by myself.* I looked around at the gifts waiting to be wrapped. *And poor them. Those people in the hospital. Among strangers. These gifts are supposed to make them feel better—how could I have thought about ruining them, even for a second?! That would have been so mean of me when they're having a tough time anyway, away from home and family and friends . . . like me.* I looked at the untouched ribbon and tinsel and bows on the table. *I will wrap these presents. And not only will I wrap them, but I'll wrap them really, really beautifully, so that the faces of the sick people will light up when they see them. That will show Old Croniebutt. He won't be expecting that! Ha! He thinks that he knows me, but he doesn't. Nobody does. I used to be caring once. I used to have friends! Yes. I ca-aaaa-aan b . . . be (sob, sob) n . . . ni-iiiice. N . . . NOBODY (sob, sob) u . . .understands m . . . m . . . meeeeeeeeee.*

After a good cry, I started my task with renewed enthusiasm and found that my old talent for making gifts look special soon came back. To get myself even more in the mood, I sang Christmas carols at the top of my lungs. Minutes went by as I tied and glued and cut and pasted. Hours. I lost track of time as I worked away, and the pile of unwrapped presents decreased.

When I'd finished wrapping all of the gifts, I didn't press the buzzer to let Dr. Cronus know. Instead I set about perfecting the finishing touches. Then tweaking and adding bits and pieces until every gift looked completely unique—a work of art with paper flowers and leaves and bows and twirls of colored ribbon and tape. The fancy gift wrapper in the swankiest store in Paris couldn't have done a better job.

As I was twirling a piece of silver ribbon into a double bow, the door opened, and Dr. Cronus stuck his head in. He looked at the pile of gifts stacked neatly to the left of the room. "Wow!" he said.

"Good, aren't they?" I said with a smile.

He walked in and examined a couple of the boxes on top. "No. Not good. They're *astonishing*!" He turned and looked at me. "Look what you're capable of. Just look! What happened, Leonora? What happened to make you so angry with the world?" He was looking at me with such kindness in his eyes that, for a moment, I forgot that he was one of my captors. I felt a fresh wave of sadness rushing up to the surface.

"You can tell me, Leonora," the doctor urged. "Let it out . . ."

"I . . . I . . . Poppy died. Our house over here was sold soon after," I said. "Too many memories, Mom and Dad said. We moved to the Caribbean, but nothing was the same again. Life for me lost its color. And so did Christmas." I sighed, and I was *almost* in tears again, but then I remembered that Cronus *wasn't* my friend, and I had made a vow not to ever let any of them see me cry. I shook the sad feelings away and made myself put my inner wall back up. "But that was then, and this is now."

"You had a happy home," said the doctor. "A happy life. And now I am going to let you in on a great secret, one of life's greatest lessons, and if you can learn it, your time on this earth will be marvelous. It doesn't need to be over just because life dealt you some difficult cards. Life is what *you* make it. Just like making a movie. In fact, you write, you direct, and you act in *your* own movie. The movie of your life. Never forget that. You still have a say in it all. Okay, one of the characters is gone. Your sister, Poppy. But you're still here. But what part are you playing now? Do you *like* the character you have written for yourself? This brat princess that the others call you? Do you like your script? The dialogue that you have given yourself? If you were watching yourself now on a screen, would you be proud of your part?"

"Oh, God, not more psychobabble," I groaned. "Pul-*leese*."

Dr. Cronus let out one of his sighs. "I repeat. You are the writer, the director, and the actor in your own play," he said. "It is always up to you what you make of it, just as it is up to you what you make of your month as a Zodiac Girl. And now you can go and join the others. I think that they may be having a carol session since, don't forget, it's Christmas."

I got up and left the room. *Okay*, I thought, *I write my own character? So? Yeah. I'm Leonora Hedley-Dent. Rich girl. Pretty great part, if you ask me. I have a life that people envy when I'm not stuck in this awful place. I do . . . don't I?* But seeing the footage of Poppy and remembering my Christmases gone by had made me think. I felt strange, like some of the anger had gone out of me and had been replaced by an overwhelming sense of sadness. I didn't know which was worse. Anger or sadness. When I was angry, at least I could blame everyone else. But this new feeling. This emptiness. I didn't know what to do with it. Who to direct it at.

Christmas, I said to myself. *Bah humbug!*

Chapter Twelve
Christmas present

"We don't want her with us," said Jake, as I came out of the front door to find the others from the lodge hunched around a campfire with Mr. O., Miss Loony Petunie, and Mario. Although I didn't show it, I was pleased to see that Mr. O. was still around. He seemed back to his sunny self and was busy roasting marshmallows. The others were each wearing a pair of reindeer's antlers, a warm coat, and a gloomy expression. If I hadn't felt so miserable, I might have laughed.

"And *I* don't want to be here," I said, "but Cronie Baby says that there might be a Christmas breakfast for you all if I cooperate. So what's going on out here?"

"As a special treat, ha, excuse me while I laugh," droned Marilyn, "Mario made us build this fire so that we could sit around and sing Christmas carols."

Selene got up and handed me a pair of felt antlers. I was about to object and then remembered that I had to cooperate or no fancy food tomorrow. I took them, put them on, and sat at the edge of the circle. *My "Fool of the Year" look is now complete,* I thought. *Curly hair, brown eyes, navy sweatsuit, and now antlers. And to think that only a few weeks ago, I was the queen of style.*

I looked around the campfire. Marilyn, Lynn, Jake, and Mark's faces were pink from the glow of the fire. Each of them looked far away, probably lost in their own memories of Christmases gone by. The atmosphere felt sad. Even Mark's usual scowl had been replaced by a look of regret.

How has it come to this? I asked myself. I never in a million trillion billion years thought that, at the age of 14, I'd be apart from Mommy and Daddy on Christmas Eve, of all nights. I rubbed Poppy's locket between my finger and thumb again, needing to know that it was there. It had been hers. She had been wearing it on the day that she died. The nurses gave it to us in a clear plastic bag along with her Little Mermaid watch, her blue bead bracelet, and her inhaler. I had put on the locket and hadn't taken it off since that day. Not once. Not even in the shower. At the thought of that little bag of her belongings, I felt tears spill out of my eyes and down my cheeks. I quickly brushed them away before anyone saw them. *If only,* I thought. *If only I'd behaved differently that day. If only. If only. If only I could turn back time and make it right, I would, because her death was all my fault. I am such a bad person. And I will never forgive myself, ever.*

I glanced around again. One more week to go. And deck the halls with boughs of holly, tra-la-la-la-la, la-la-la-laaaaaah.

As we sat staring into the embers of the fire and chewing on the marshmallows that Mr. O. handed out, there was the familiar roar of Hermie's motorcycle, and a few moments later he appeared and skidded to a halt in front of the fire. Even he had made an effort for Christmas, and his usual garb of black leather was adorned with garlands of tinsel. He reached into the box on the back of his motorcycle and pulled out five packages. "I bring greetings from the outside world," he said as he handed them over to us. "Jake, Marilyn, Lynn, Mark, and . . . yep, one for you, Leonora."

Everyone was silent as they tore off the wrapping paper.

Mark's package contained a video phone. Jake got a card and a box of chocolates, which he immediately opened and passed around. They tasted like heaven. Lynn got a pink wool scarf, which she wrapped around her neck. And Marilyn got a card with a photo and a bunch of CDs.

"What did you get?" asked Lynn.

I looked down at the box on my knee. It was a portable DVD player. And a DVD.

Hermie pointed at a switch. "That's the 'on' button," he said.

"I know," I said.

"What is it?" asked Jake. "A Christmas movie to pass the time? Can we all watch?"

"It's a message from your mom and dad," Hermie said.

I sat and looked at the DVD player. It felt like it was a bomb waiting to go off. *What if the DVD was a movie with Poppy in it and the others ask me about her?* I wondered. *What will I say?* I was about to hide it when Mr. O. shook his head.

"I think we should all share what we've received tonight," he said. "In the spirit of Christmas, I'd like to hear what you've received and what it means to you."

There was a collective groan. "Noooooooooo."

Mr. O. clapped his hands. "Okay, then let's play a game first. Role reversal."

There was another collective groan. "Noooooooooo."

Mr. O. paid no attention to any of us. "Okay. Who should we have go first?"

"Leonora," said Marilyn. "It's only fair, since she messed up dinner for us."

I knew that I had to cooperate. If I didn't, there would be no breakfast. Plus, I was starting to get tired of being so objectionable *all* the time. I'd show them. I *could* play nice. "Okay. Who do you want me to be?"

Mr. O. beamed and gave me the thumbs-up. "You can play your mother," he said. "And . . . Marilyn, you can be Leonora."

Marilyn leaped up. "Love to," she said and immediately put a really sour expression on her face.

"I don't do that," I said.

"You *soooo* do," chorused Lynn, Jake, and Mark.

Marilyn started flouncing around like a total drama queen. "I am so superior. I don't know whaaaat I am doing here with these losers. Oh, loser," she turned to Selene, "get me a grilled cheese, would you? And make it snappy." Then she turned to Mark. "And, slave boy, get me a goose-down comforter, would you? I am sooooo cold. Brrr. Never mind the others. Who cares about them. Oh, me me me me me me me. Oh, my hair! It's all curly. Oh. I think I might die. And that shampoo? It's like sooooooo last century."

The others cracked up laughing. Not me, though. I felt *outraged*.

"Go on, Leonora," urged Mr. O. "Be your mom. You can do it."

I felt like my legs had turned to concrete, but I forced myself to move. *You can do this*, I told myself. *If there's one thing I can do better than anything, that's act. My life since Poppy died has all been an act.* "Now then, sweetheart . . ." I began as I got up.

Marilyn turned and gave me a scathing look. "I'm not your sweetheart. I'm nobody's sweetheart, and I'll be suing your sorry butt as soon as I get out of here."

Jake fell down laughing.

148

"But it's for your own good, dear," I said in Mommy's gentle voice, and even if I say so myself, I had it down pretty well. Drama was my best subject in school, even before my talent for figuring out interest in math class. I glanced at Mr. O., and he gave me an encouraging wink.

Marilyn folded her arms and pinched in her mouth. "You're not my mother. I disown you. I *hate* you."

It was so weird, because when she said that she hated me, it hurt. "No, darling, please don't . . ."

"Oh, don't simper, Mommy. You're like . . . so . . . *annoying*. Like, excuse you for squeaking," snapped Marilyn as she stepped forward and gave me a good push, so forceful that I fell back into a bush. That hurt too, and as I lay there, I realized that pushing someone into a bush was exactly what I had done to Daddy on the day I left to board the plane just three weeks ago.

"Okay, well done, girls," said Selene. "Yes. Um. Enough now. Come on, Leonora. Up you come." She got up and came over to where I lay and offered me her hand.

"Just give me a minute," I said. "Please." I lay in the bush and closed my eyes. A hundred tantrums I'd had in the past year flashed through my mind. The hurtful words I had said to Mommy and Daddy. The moods. The slammed doors. Phone calls cut short. I opened my eyes to see Marilyn still flouncing around being brat princess *à la* Leonora Hedley-Dent, and I thought about what old Cronus had just said about life being like a movie. Well, if that was true, I might have the lead role in my personal movie, but my character stank. *She needs a major rewrite*, I thought as I pulled a twig out of my hair and continued looking up at the black sky. *I have been the daughter from hell. No wonder Mommy and Daddy sent me here.*

A few moments later I scrambled out of the bush, and Mr. O. patted the ground next to him to indicate that I should go and sit by him.

"Okay?" he asked as I took my place.

I nodded, but I felt peculiar—as if I was waking from a long, stressful dream.

We played out some more scenarios. Lynn got to be Dr. Cronus, which she did very well—grumping and scowling her way around the campfire and threatening us all with extra lessons. Mark got to be Selene, and he played her as a madwoman who lived her life by the phases of the Moon and who liked to do strange dances to "get her feelings out." Mark was turning out to be a lot of fun since he'd started talking, and Selene took his impersonation like a great sport and laughed along with the rest of us.

When the role-playing had finished, Selene asked to see what we had all gotten in our packages.

"You go first, Jake," he said.

Jake held up sticky fingers. "Chocolates. They're my favorite. Mom always gets them for me for Christmas." He showed us the card that accompanied the box of chocolates. Inside it was a photo of a boy who looked like a younger version of Jake. He had a sweet face and was in a hospital bed. His parents were on each side, and the boy was holding up a teddy bear with a Santa hat on it. It made me think of all the times that my family had accompanied Poppy to the hospital when she couldn't breathe and that last fateful time when she didn't come home with us. I glanced at Jake's earnest face and hoped that he never had to go through the same thing.

"What's the matter with your brother?" I asked.

Jake shrugged. "Some kind of autoimmune disease, I think it's called."

"Can they help him?" I asked.

Jake shook his head. "Not here, they can't. They could if we sent him to America. There's a man there who could help him, but we can't afford it."

"Is that why you stole cars?" asked Selene.

Jake nodded. "Yeah. Partially. I was trying to raise the money. But . . . I enjoyed it, too. It was a laugh. Something to do to take my mind off things."

Mario got up and stood threateningly over Jake. "But you won't be doing that type of thing anymore, *will* you?"

Jake coughed. "Um, no. 'Course not, sir."

"Good," said Mario. "Because, if you do, you'll be back here before you can say BMW. Your choice. So who's next? Mark?"

Mark showed us his video phone. His family had recorded a message for him, and he showed us a busy family scene, with dogs, cats, babies, grandparents, parents, siblings. All the adults were singing "We Wish You a Merry Christmas." They looked like a lot of fun.

"They must have all pitched in to get it for me," said Mark. "I would have stolen it from somewhere if I'd been home, probably." Then he coughed and glanced at Mario. "But not anymore, sir. No, sir. I have mended my ways. Sir."

We all laughed.

"Sounds like your family knows how to enjoy Christmas," said Selene.

Mark nodded. "Yeah. I guess so. Might be the last one in that house, though. Come the new year, they're going to be evicted. The landlord raised the rent. My dad lost his job. My mom has done everything that she can, but no luck. My family will be homeless."

"Maybe something will turn up," said Selene. "You never know what's around the next corner."

"Yes, I do. Homelessness," snapped Mark, and he punched his right palm with his left hand. "And there's *nothing* I can do about it. Not in here where the stupid social services sent me."

Oh, God, here we go with the sob stories again, I thought when I noticed that Mr. O. was giving me a very pointed look.

"What?" I asked.

"And what do you think of Mark's situation?" he asked.

I shrugged. "Yeah. Tough. Win some, lose some."

Mr. O. looked at me with narrowed eyes and then sighed heavily. Whatever he was thinking, it wasn't happy thoughts.

"What did you get, Lynn?" asked Selene.

"A scarf from Mom. She wouldn't send a photo. Not of her and *him*. She knows how I feel about my stepfather, but . . ."

"And how do you feel about him?" Selene asked.

Lynn shifted around and then stared at her feet. "I guess . . . well, sometimes people deserve a second chance, don't they?"

When she said that, we all knew that she was talking about herself and not just her mom or her stepfather. And then I noticed that Mr. O. was giving me his pointed look again.

"What? *What?*" I asked.

Mr. O. just pouted as a reply. *He's such a drama queen,* I thought. "I'm not psychic," I said. "If you're trying to tell me something, just tell me."

"Ha!" said Mr. O. "*Now* she wants to listen. Honestly! In all my days I have never had one like you."

"What do you mean?" I asked.

"One who ignores me like *you* do. Really. Leos can

be self-centered at the best of times, but *you*! You take the prize. Leonora—it's *clear* what you have to do. But have you listened? Learned anything? Oh, no. First you smash your phone, and then you rip up all my messages. All that good advice I've been sending you. All in the garbage. Don't think that I don't know."

Oops, I thought. "Oh, that. Yeah. I know. Um . . . sorry? Um. I will try to be better. Is that what you want to hear? Is that why you're giving me those looks?"

Mr. O. sighed heavily. "I give up," he said, and then he turned to the others. "This time here could have changed everything for Leonora, but I fear she's going to blow it by being stubborn. It does happen sometimes. Not often. Most girls are over the Moon to be a Zodiac Girl. Okay, sometimes it takes some adjusting to, but never, *never* before have I had one who rejects the whole idea *and* breaks her phone."

"Ooh, dear," I said. "Listen to you. Just because you're not the center of attention, you don't like it. Honestly, the way you go on, you really do think that everything revolves around you, don't you?"

There was an awkward silence, and then Selene coughed. "Well, it does actually . . . He *is* the Sun."

"Okay," said Mark. "Enough. What is all this? Maybe someone can explain. This zodiac thing? Even that deli guy who was here with the food was going on about it. He called you a Zodiac Girl, Leonora. What's it all

154

about, exactly?"

"Every month, somewhere on the planet, a girl is chosen to be a Zodiac Girl . . ." Selene began. I glanced at Mr. O. He seemed to have gone into a major sulk, which made me want to smile. I was beginning to feel very fond of him. He could stick his bottom lip out farther than I could.

"Chosen how?" asked Lynn.

"Different elements every time," Selene continued. "The only thing that each Zodiac Girl has in common is that it happens at a turning point in her life, and for one month, she gets the help of the planets."

I sighed. I knew that there was no hiding the fact that I was this month's Zodiac Girl any longer. "Blah blah de blah. Oh, come on, surely I'm not the only one who has heard them going on about the Moon and the stars, and Mr. O. saying that he is the Sun."

"Yeah, but I thought he was speaking metaphorically," said Marilyn. "You know, like 'e's a little ray of sunshine and all that."

I shook my head. "Nope. He thinks he *is* the Sun. As in the planet. Don't you, Mr. O.?"

Mr. O. stuck out his bottom lip even farther while Jake burst out laughing. "No way," he said.

"Yeah. No way. You're saying to me that Mr. O. said that he was the manifestation of the Sun?" asked Lynn. "Do you think that, Mr. O.? Do you?"

"I'm not saying anything," said Mr. O. "In fact, I may not stay around if I'm not going to be appreciated."

He got up and flounced off into the dark garden. Mario, Selene, and Hermie rushed after him, and we could hear them reasoning with him a distance away. I could just about make out "She's not going to change." "Some you just have to accept are stuck in their ways . . ."

"It's not just him," I continued. "Loony Petunie thinks she's the Moon, Dr. Cronus thinks he's Saturn, Mario is Mars, and Hermie is apparently none other than Mercury, the planet of communication here in earthly form as a motorcycle messenger boy."

Marilyn rolled her eyes to the sky. "Pff. Yeah, right."

"Are you kidding us?" asked Mark.

I shook my head. "Honest. That's what they think."

Lynn looked troubled. "Oh. My. God. I thought there was something different about them, but I thought that it was you, me, Mark, Lynn, and Marilyn who were supposed to need help."

"I know! Do you think that our parents know that they signed us away to a bunch of crazies?" asked Marilyn.

"Probably not," said Lynn. "But . . . how come no one's mentioned any of this zodiac stuff to the rest of us? Only to you."

"Not just me. Dr. Cronus goes on about it just about every day in classes," I said.

"Yeah, I guess . . . but I thought that was just a lesson

in astronomy, and no one listens to 'im much anyway, and 'e didn't say much about you being a Zodiac Girl," said Marilyn, as behind her Mr. O., Mario, Selene, and Hermie returned to the fire.

Jake leaned over and whispered, "If what Leonora is saying is true or even half true, best play along—not let on that we know they need to be locked up, right?"

Mark, Marilyn, and Lynn quickly nodded and assumed their usual blank expressions.

"It's all true!" boomed Mr. O. "We are the planets, and Leonora is a Zodiac Girl. Every case is different depending on the needs of the girl in question, but never before has someone so ruthlessly rejected our help!"

"Okay. So what does Leonora need, then?" asked Jake. "Maybe we can help."

Mr. O. glared at him for a second, as if doubting his sincerity, but then he sat down cross-legged by the campfire. "Only she can discover that," he said. "I was only here to guide and advise. But if she won't listen, what can I do?"

"I'll listen," I said. If listening meant breakfast, I could do that no problem, plus I had genuinely grown to like Mr. O., crazy or not. "And I'm sorry if I've been rude. Yeah. I am. Really."

Mr. O. looked at me very closely, as if he was trying to gauge if I was being sincere. I looked back at him and smiled.

He looked taken aback but smiled in return. "Hmm," he said.

"So, please, what's next on my zodiac agenda?" I asked.

"Neptune," he said.

"*Neptune.* That's a new one. I don't think that you've mentioned that before," I said, doing my best to look as enthusiastic as I could.

Mr. O. still looked a little suspicious.

"So what's Neptune all about?" I asked.

"You really want to know?"

I nodded.

"Mystery," said Mr. O. "Illusion. Neptune governs the realm where nothing is really what it seems. The realm of dreams, in fact."

"Can't wait," I said. "And when will I get to meet him, or is it a her?"

"Him," said Mr. O. "Tonight. Neptune is in conjunction with Pluto at an angle to—"

"Two of them. A double whammy," Lynn interrupted. "Lucky you, Leonora."

"So, what's Pluto about?" asked Marilyn, with a sly wink at me. I winked back. Mario Mars couldn't accuse me of not being a team player now. We were backing each other up perfectly.

"Pluto is the planet of transformation," said Mr. O.

"Impressive," said Jake.

"He is," said Selene. "Where Pluto is in your birth chart can determine matters of life or death."

"Life or death, huh?" said Lynn. "Sounds ser . . . ious." She almost blew it by laughing on the last line, but she caught herself just in time.

"So are these guys coming to the lodge?" I asked.

"It is up to them how or when they choose to make themselves known to you," said Mr. O.

"Sounds spooky," said Marilyn. "You just give us a shout if you need a hand, Leonora."

I felt touched by her offer to help. It was the kindest gesture she'd made since I had arrived at the lodge. "What did you get in your package?" I asked and put on my best "I am really interested" look. Mr. O. continued staring at me, so I turned and winked at him. He looked more confused than ever.

Marilyn showed us the photo of her mom. She was around 40, with short, dark hair and a kind but sad face. Marilyn looked wistful as she showed it, and I wondered if she was regretting how she'd behaved toward her mom in the past, just as I was beginning to regret the way that I'd acted with my parents.

And then it was my turn. I so hoped that Mom or Dad didn't say anything that gave anything away. Poppy was my secret, and, even after all that had happened, I wasn't ready to share her with the group.

They hated me enough as it was. They'd only hate me more when they found out what I'd done. I took a deep breath and turned on the DVD player.

Mommy and Daddy's image filled the seven-inch frame.

Mommy looked tearful, and then she took a deep breath and began to speak. "Darling Leo, we've only been given a minute to talk to you on here, so I'll make it quick. I just wanted to say that I love you very much. And I always will."

Next to her, Daddy nodded.

"We regret that we had to take such severe measures," Mommy continued, "but felt we had no other option. None of us could continue as we were."

"And, Leonora," Daddy interrupted, "we want you to know that we don't blame you. We never have. It wasn't your fault, and you must not blame yourself. We love you now, and we have always have and—"

"—we hope to see you very soon," Mommy finished for him.

For a few seconds it felt like I was home, where I belonged, but then the screen went fuzzy and then black, and I was back around a campfire with a bunch of strangers outside a lodge in the middle of nowhere on Christmas Eve on a cold, cold night. The sense of belonging that I had felt earlier faded away like warm breath in the air on a freezing night, and I made myself put my inner wall back up, stronger than ever.

And then the inevitable questions came.

"What must you not blame yourself for?" asked Lynn.

"What did you do?" asked Mark.

"What don't they blame you for?" asked Jake.

"Nothing. For being a pain, probably," I said. It was a half truth. I couldn't tell the whole story. No one knew that. Not even Mommy and Daddy. And no one would ever understand. *Mommy and Daddy can say that they don't blame me,* I thought, as the fire grew dim and the others grew sleepy, *but they don't know what really happened on the day that Poppy died. Only I know that, and I can never forgive myself.*

When I got back to the dorm, I wrote another letter:

Dear Mommy and Daddy,

I am miserable. Please let me out. Everyone hates me. I hate myself. I know that I am bad, but I will try to change. I am sorry about everything.

Yours,

Leonora

Chapter Thirteen
Christmas Future

I was in a hospital room. There was an empty bed. A man and a woman were putting clothes and things into a suitcase. Where was I? In the hospital where Poppy was? No. It wasn't there, although the man and woman looked familiar. Not my mom and dad, though. No. It was *Jake's* mom and dad. What was I doing watching them? How did I get there? And where was his younger brother?

A man with a white beard and what appeared to be a broom walked in. "You're dreaming," he said, and his broom turned into a trident, like the one that you see the king of the sea carrying. At least you do on the bags that Mommy used to get our fish and chips in when we lived in England in our country house. The place that she went to was called Poseidon. I think he was the king of the sea. It was then that I remembered why the village of Osbury had seemed familiar when we had driven through it on the way up to the lodge. *Of course. That's it!* I thought as it came back to me. It was where Mom used to go shopping and get her hair done. I *knew*

I had been there before.

"Who are you?" I asked.

"The planet Neptune," he said.

"Ah, yes. I was told to expect you. You rule the realm of dreams, right?"

The old man nodded.

"Cool. I've met some of your friends already," I continued. "So where's Jake's brother?"

Neptune shook his head. "He didn't make it."

"What do you mean, *didn't make it?* " I gasped.

Neptune acted out someone's throat being cut.

"You mean kaput?" I asked.

He nodded and disappeared, and then a moment later, another figure appeared. He looked like a handsome goth prince. Younger than the king of the sea. He was tall, dressed in black with a pale, long face, and hair tied back in a ponytail. He bowed. "Leonora. At your service. I'm P. J."

"Pluto?"

"Indeed. Some call me P. J., but I am also known as Pluto, ze great renewer."

"Excellent. And I'm dreaming, apparently. Is that why Jake's parents haven't noticed me?"

P. J. nodded. "Zey can't see you."

"So why are you here?"

"I've been sent to help wiz your transformation. To show you a few things."

"Like what?" I asked. I was enjoying the encounter with him and Neptune. I felt like I was floating and everything was unreal.

"Like your future."

"Oh, okay. But what about Jake's brother? Is what happens to him part of my future?"

"Zat depends on you."

That made me feel confused, and I tried to make myself wake up, but it didn't seem to be happening. P. J. beckoned for me to follow him out of the room.

It was weird. I walked out through the door, but instead of finding a hospital corridor, we were out in a small room in what appeared to be a shabby hotel. I could see through a grimy window that it was raining outside. In a room of the hotel there was a family eating a takeout pizza. They also looked familiar. I soon recognized them. They were Mark's family, complete with cat, but they didn't look as happy as they had on Mark's video phone. Even the cat looked fed up. A middle-aged woman looked like she had been crying, and the man with her— who, I presumed, was Mark's dad—looked like he had the weight of the world on his shoulders. It made me feel sad just looking at them. *It's a dream, a dream*, I told myself, although it was beginning to feel more like a *bad* dream. *Not my responsibility. Thank God my family at least has a home, several in fact, and food and lots of money.*

"Hey, P. J., my man," I said. "Charming though you

are, why are you showing me the future of my fellow inmates but not what's ahead for me?"

"Look, Leonora, look again. Zeir future iz tied wiz yours."

"Yeah, right." I laughed. "I don't think so. Me, rich. They, poor. I will be going home to a very nice house with servants, and these people . . . well . . ."

"Homeless," said P. J. in a flat voice. "Zey are in a hostel for ze homeless."

"Whatever. So what's next on the agenda? The starving people in Africa?"

P. J. gave me a disgusted look. As if what he'd been showing me was *my* fault. "Don't you care, Leonora?"

"Yeah. 'Course. But for one thing, this is a *dream*. And in real life, there are people who work to help the poor, aren't there? Charities. Social workers. In case you hadn't noticed, I'm a fourteen-year-old girl. What can I do?"

"More zan most fourteen year olds, zat's for sure," P. J. said, and I got a strong feeling that he didn't like me. I made a face at him as he beckoned me on. I was glad that Mr. O. was my guardian and not this intense-looking misery.

"I am so not interested. Come on, then, show me something impressive. Show me *my* future."

P. J. paused for a second as if considering my request, and then he beckoned me on. "You asked for it," he said.

We left Mark's family behind, walked through the door of the hostel, and found ourselves in a store. A scruffy store full of all types of things: clothes, shoes, toys, curtains, pots, pans—in fact, it looked like . . . a thrift store! I'd never been inside of one before but had seen them from the outside. *What am I doing in here?* I wondered. It felt so peculiar. *Remember, you are dreaming,* I reminded myself as I looked around and saw . . .

Noooooooooooooooooo! No. No. No. No. NOOOOOOO.

This time it wasn't the people who looked familiar. It was the stuff on sale. Racks and racks of what looked like *MY* clothes. And my shoes! And people were pawing over them like they were on sale! *No waaaaay*, I thought. Of all the things I'd seen, this had to be the worst.

"These are *my* things!" I said as I tried to pull a pair of shoes out of a woman's hand. To no avail, my hands went right through her. And then I noticed the price on the shoes. Five dollars! *Totally freaky!*

I fell to my knees. "Oh, P. J., please. Make this stop. Come on, this isn't a dream anymore. This is a *nightmare*. Those shoes are labeled five dollars. They're by Jimmy Choo, and they're worth eight hundred!" I tried to say, "Noooo, leave my things alone" to the woman holding the shoes, but she couldn't hear me. It was as if my mouth was full of a huge wad of gum. It was only when I spoke to P. J. that my words came out properly, and he looked like he was finding the whole scene very amusing.

"Don't you vonder vhy your clozing iz here?" he asked.

"Yeah. No." I felt confused. "It's not real, is it? Like, not really happening? Like, a dream, right?"

"Sometimes our dreams show uz our future," said P. J.

I felt a shiver of dread go up my spine. "And you're saying that my clothes will be on sale in some secondhand store? No. *Never.* Mommy and Daddy would never allow it. Nooooooo. Why would they? Please. Not this. Don't show me this. Anything but this."

P. J. chuckled and then beckoned me into a dressimg room. I got up to follow him, wondering what horrors awaited me in there. Some beggar in one of my "Chanel teen" dresses? Some stinky poor person in one of my Versace tops? It was too, *too* horrible. But no. P. J. and I were in a church. There was the sound of a choir. A few people in pews. In the center was a coffin covered with white roses.

These people were the most familiar of all. In the front pew were Mommy and Daddy. A wave of joy flooded through me.

"Mommy, Daddy!" I cried, but they didn't even look up.

"Zey can't hear you, remember?" P. J. reminded me.

And there were Shirla, Mason, and Henry in the second row. And my darling Coco, her fur back to its natural white color.

"Oh, no, P. J., please. Don't show me Poppy's funeral."

"Not Poppy's," said P. J., and with a snap of his fingers, we were outside. We were in a cemetery. My parents were there again, under a green umbrella that almost blew inside out in the gale. Rain lashed down, but it didn't touch me. Shirla and Henry and Mason were standing with my parents under a second huge umbrella. I looked at the gravestone. It *was* Poppy's grave. I remembered it well. The engraving of her name had been etched in my heart as well as on the stone. Beloved daughters . . . WAIT a minute! Beloved *daughters*? As in plural! Poppy Hedley-Dent and . . . Leonora Hedley-DENT!!!!!! Leonora. Hedley. Dent. That was me. That was *my* grave! My name. Noooooooooo. It couldn't be. Not me. Not dead. Not six feet under! *No. No. It's a dream*, I told myself again. *Mr. O. warned me. Neptune. An encounter with the planet where things are not as they appear to be. And Pluto, the planet that deals with life and death.*

"Ha! They're not even crying," I said as I turned to P. J. "Surely they'd cry just a little? Hey. You're not death, are you?"

"Some people might say zat I am. I am Pluto, and if you don't mind, I don't like ze word 'death.' I prefer ze words 'mortally challenged.' "

I almost laughed. "A politically-correct phantom. Oh, get a life, will you?"

P. J. gave me a scathing look. "You may laugh, but

you should listen to me. I don't just deal in death. I deal in ze transformation."

"So you keep telling me. Look, man, P. J., Pluto, or whoever, I'm having a really bad dream, and I'd like you to butt out of it, if you don't mind. I . . ." I pointed at the gravestone. "That's my grave down there. Well, not exactly, it's not . . . because I'm up here, but . . . look here, I'd like to go back to the dorm now and wake up. For this to be over."

P. J. nodded. "To dream about death doesn't necessarily mean a physical death. It can be symbolic. Like ze end of something."

"Whatever. Yeah, but *was* that really my future? Is that what's going to happen, or only what *might* happen?"

"Maybe it signifies ze end of something, Leonora."

"The end of what? What?"

"Listen to vot zey are saying," urged P. J., and suddenly I could hear the people by the grave—as if someone had suddenly turned up the sound on a movie.

"None of her friends showed up," said Henry.

"What friends?" asked Shirla. "She pushed them all away. No one stayed her friend for long."

Henry shook his head. "What a shame. What a lonely little girl she was."

Mason grimaced and said, "Don't feel sorry for her. She was a total brat. A brat princess. No wonder she didn't have any friends."

"What will happen to her money?" asked Shirla. "Her savings account?"

"Her parents have become so disillusioned with money and all that goes with it that they are going to give all of their and Leonora's savings away. Her clothes have already gone to the Salvation Army."

"NooooooooooooooooooooooOOOOOOOOOO," I groaned. "I HAAAATE this dream. Get me out of it!"

P.J. put a finger to his lips as if to hush me.

"At least we're off the hook, then," said Shirla. "We won't have to repay our loans plus the interest. Glory be for that!"

"Amen," said Henry. "Amen."

"I still feel sorry for her a little," said Shirla. "I think she never did get over the death of her sister."

"It's true," said Mason. "She was a sweet kid before that."

"I find that hard to believe," said Henry. "But that was before my time. What happened?"

Shirla shook her head, as if even to think about it was hard.

"Her younger sister," she said, "she had an asthma attack. Leonora, she blamed herself, although it wasn't her fault. Poor Poppy. Some nasty kid at their school had been picking on her . . . a bully . . ."

I nodded. "Mo Bolton," I whispered.

"One night, this girl and her friends, they's taunting young Poppy on her way home. She starts to have an asthma attack, and Mo runs off with the inhaler, laughing like crazy, not realizing that, without it, the poor girl couldn't breathe."

I felt tears come to my eyes. "That was my fault, *my* fault. I should have been there."

"Vhy vas it your fault, Leonora?" asked P. J. "It vasn't you who ran off wiz the inhaler. You loved Poppy."

A crippling pain hit my stomach, and I buckled over. "Enough. Don't make me talk about this. Think about this. I fear *this* more than anything else. Please, let it go. Let me wake up now."

"You can tell me," said P. J. "I'm not real. It iz only a dream, remember. Only a dream, so no one else vill ever know vot you say. It's just between you and me."

I felt my head begin to spin and was finding it hard to breathe, dream or no dream.

"I . . . I . . . can't . . ."

"Leonora, talk to me. You can tell me everyzing. Leonora, you must let it out."

I crumpled to my knees on the floor. Without looking at P. J.'s face, I began to tell him what happened on that fateful night.

"We went home together after school every day. Mo Bolton didn't bother her when I was around. She wouldn't dare. I could handle her easily. But that day . . ." I felt a huge sob come into my throat, like a bubble stuck there, blocking my speech.

"Go on, Leonora," P. J. urged.

I forced myself to breathe. ". . . my friend Jasmine, she wanted to go to the mall, and I wanted to go with her. 'Course Poppy wanted to come with us, but I said no."

"Why did you say no, Leonora?"

"I was . . . I was worried that Jasmine wasn't my friend anymore. She'd been spending more and more time with another girl in our class, and I . . . I wanted to make sure we were still best friends. Jasmine was my best friend and one of the most popular girls in our class. I really wanted to stay friends with her because it meant that I was popular too. So I told Poppy to go home on her own. It wasn't far. Our school was only at the end of our street, but . . . I shouldn't have let her go. She was crying, and I told her to grow up and stop acting like a crybaby. Mo and her friends were hiding."

"Had zat ever happened before, Leonora?"

I shook my head. "Mo lived on the other side of town. I don't know what she was doing on our street."

"And had Poppy ever gone home on her own before?" P. J. asked.

I nodded. "Sometimes. Not often, though. I usually went with her, but that night . . . it was as if she had an instinct that something was going to happen. Mo

172

had threatened her during the day. We never got to find out about it because Mo was taken to a special school afterward. All types of people came out after Poppy's death and said what a bully Mo was. But it was too late by then. Too late for my sister. I felt mean not letting her go with me, but I . . . I wanted to stay friends with Jas. If only, if only I . . ." And then a dam burst inside of me. All of the tears that I had been holding back came flooding through like an avalanche.

P. J. placed his hand on my back and let me sob my heart out to him.

"I'm so sorry. *So* sorry. Don't you understand now? It was . . . my . . . fault, and my last words to her were to scram. That she was . . . a silly crybaby. I didn't want her around. You should have seen her face. Like I'd b . . . b . . . broken her heart. That face has stayed with . . . me . . . forever."

P. J. gently stroked my hair. "You poor, poor child," he said. "Poor, poor child."

And that set me off crying again. I knew I didn't deserve anyone to be nice to me. Anyone calling me a poor child and stroking my hair. I was evil. Hateful. The worst person alive.

"After Poppy's death, I thought that I would never let anyone close again, so I put up a wall. Made myself not care. I wouldn't let anyone in."

"Understandable," said P. J. in a gentle voice.

P. J. let me cry until there were no tears left. And nothing more to say. Just a feeling of complete and utter exhaustion. I felt like I hadn't slept for a million years. *But I was asleep, wasn't I? Wasn't I? It was all a dream.*

"Am I still dreaming?" I asked.

"Look around you," said P. J. and, when I did so, I saw that I was in the dorm, back in my narrow bed at the lodge. I opened my eyes and sat up. P. J. was sitting at the foot of the bed. From the other side of the room came the sounds of gentle breathing and Lynn snoring. Both girls were asleep.

"Zey can't see me," said P. J. "Or hear uz. It iz only a dream."

"But how are you here now in reality as well as then in my dream?"

"To make sure you understood vot you saw, Leonora."

"I don't think I understand *anything* anymore," I said. It was all so extraordinary. However, I couldn't deny that I felt better having told someone what had happened with Poppy, even if P. J. was a figment of my imagination.

"I can see vhy you feel so bad about your sister's death," he said, "but zere was nozing you could have done. It vas her time. If she hadn't gone zat way, she vould have gone anozer. Zere vas nozing you could do. You must understand zat. But here . . ." He indicated the sleeping shapes of Lynn and Marilyn. "Here zere's

174

a lot you can do."

"What do you mean?"

"Zink about it. Remember vat you've dreamed tonight. You'll find a vay. You vill, for in your heart, you're not a bad girl, Leonora Hedley-Dent."

And when he said that, I felt like crying again.

Chapter Fourteen
Christmas wishes

"And a merry Christmas to you," groaned Lynn when the lights blasted on.

I leaped out of bed. "And a *merry* Christmas to you," I said, and I meant it. I felt totally, absolutely, amazingly wonderful.

Lynn and Marilyn both threw their pillows at me. "Shut up, will you?" they moaned in unison.

I felt like dancing, so I did. An Irish jig at the foot of the bed.

"Come on," I said to the girls as the door opened and Mark poked his head around. "Get up. It's Christmas Day."

"But you don't *do* Christmas, remember?" said Marilyn.

Mark came in and sat at the foot of Lynn's bed, and he was soon joined by Jake. "Yeah. Are you on *drugs*, Leonora?" he asked.

I felt so good that I hugged myself. "Nope. Just high on . . . life! God, it's good to be alive!" I stood on my head, just for the heck of it. When I saw the others' faces, I burst out laughing. Jake, Mark, Marilyn, and Lynn were sitting up, gawping at me with their mouths open.

"Aliens were here last night, and they ate your brain—didn't they?" asked Jake.

"Jake. Jakey baby. Jake, my man. My friend," I said and then did a cartwheel down the middle of the aisle between the beds and landed neatly at the end of Lynn's bed and gave him a hug. "Merry Christmas."

He pushed me off. "Get off. You're *frightening* me!"

I went over and hugged Mark. He pushed me off too. "Cut the vomit stuff, brat princess. I don't buy it. What's the game? Is this some new trick to get out of here? Jake's already done the crazy act. It didn't work. No point in you trying it too . . . although I have to say that you're a lot more convincing than Jake was."

"Do you think we should ask Mario to get a doctor?" asked Marilyn. "I really think she might 'ave flipped."

I laughed again. "No. Not really. This is the season to be jolly, and I am. Jolly, that is. I feel good, no, not good, GREAT!" I began to sing. "Oh . . . jingle bells, jingle bells, jingle all the waaaaaaaay."

Lynn noticed a small pile of packages by the door. "Hey, look! Presents! Maybe they're for us!" She raced over to look, and, indeed, the names on the labels were ours. "Hooray! Presents. I *love* presents."

There were two for me and one for everyone else. I quickly unwrapped my first one to find that it was a phone similar to the phone that I'd destroyed on the first day that I'd arrived. Gold with a large diamond on it. It was actually cute, and I resolved that I wouldn't break it this time. In the second package was the chain with the lion's head on it. I'd wondered where that had gone. Mr. O. must have found it and kept it for me.

In the meantime, the others had unwrapped their packages too. Marilyn got a mug with "Taurus" written on it (that was her birth sign). Lynn got a pink baseball cap with a ram on it (she was an Aries) and a bottle of what looked like paint remover. She laughed and then rolled up a sleeve and pointed at her tattoo. "It's not real. It's one of the ones that comes off with the right remover. I got it done. I don't even like tattoos."

"So why did you put it on?" I asked.

"To make me look tough, but . . . I guess I don't need to do that anymore."

I gave her a hug. "No, you don't. We're all friends here."

"You're weird," she said. "What do you want?"

"Nothing," I replied. "To be friends, that's all."

She looked at me suspiciously, but I grinned back at her.

Mark got a tiny laptop and some computer games and a note saying, "For the next time you get bored." He looked pleased with his gift.

"What did you get, Jake?" asked Lynn.

"Same as Mark. A little laptop and a computer game.

A *car* computer game, and there's a note with it. 'It's safer to joyride these cars than real ones.' Hmm. I guess. What did you get, Leonora?"

I showed them my phone and the necklace and the girls *ooh*ed and *aah*ed. *Just imagine if they saw my collection back home*, I thought. One of my phones was made from real diamonds.

Mr. O. appeared at the door. "So, did you give each other any gifts?" he asked.

Jake snorted. "What? Like a moldy sock?"

"Or a potato?" asked Lynn. "We don't have anything to give, or hadn't you noticed?"

"Leonora . . ." said Mr. O., and he gave me the same pointed look that he had given me the previous night at the campfire.

"What?" I asked. "What am I supposed to give?" I put my hand up to my neck. "Not my locket. That's the only thing I have here."

"No one wants your stupid locket," sneered Marilyn.

Mr. O. sighed. "Your dreams, Leonora. Your encounter with Neptune and Pluto. Didn't you learn *anything* from them?"

"I . . . I . . ." I'd been so glad to wake up and realize that my dreams had been just dreams that I hadn't given them any further thought, but Mr. O. was staring at me like I'd missed something.

"Take five minutes, all of you," he said and began to

hand out paper and pens. "I thought that each of you might like to send your parents a message since it's Christmas. If you write to them, Hermie will be sure that they get them sometime today." With another pointed look in my direction, he left us alone.

I sat at thefootd of my bed, went through my dream in my mind, and racked my brain as to what it was that Mr. O. thought that I could do. As the dreams came back to me, it started to dawn on me, and I began to write my letter:

Dear Mommy and Daddy,

I am so sorry for all the trouble I have caused in the past few years. I should have been better, I know that I should. Poppy was your daughter as well as my sister, and of course you miss her as much as I do. I am sorry that I have been so selfish. It was my only way of coping, and I cut myself off from you. Can you forgive me for being such a terrible pain?

I have one more week here, and I don't mind at all. I really don't. I have more to learn here and a lot more to do.

I do love you, and I promise that when I come home, I will be a good girl. The old Leonora. I'm not the girl you sent here. I will change.

With lots of love and kisses,
Your daughter, Leo

After ten minutes, Mr. O. came back into the room and began to collect our letters. I glanced over at him, and he nodded.

"Ready, Leonora?" he asked.

I took a deep breath and nodded back to him. I knew what I had to do. "Okay, everyone, Mr. O. was right before. I do have some gifts that I'd like to give you. First for you, Jake. Merry Christmas. I'd like to pay for your little brother to get the best treatment that he needs—that is, if you'll let me."

Jake's face crumpled. "Don't make fun of me, Leonora," he said. "It's not funny."

"I'm not. *Really*, I'm not, Jake. I have money. Lots of it. *Loads* of it. I don't need it all, and, well . . . my little sister was sick once, and . . . and I . . . I lost her. There was nothing I could do. But I *can* help you—that is, if you'll let me."

Jake looked around at the others as if he was trying to figure out what was happening, but they looked just as mystified as he did.

"You mean it?" Jake asked.

"I do. You have my solemn vow. Cross my heart and hope to die. I really mean it."

Jake took a long look at me, as if trying to gauge if I was messing with him, and then he thumped his forehead with the palm of his hand. "Oh, I get it. You mean you'll *lend* it to me, and you want interest?"

"*No*. NO! Honestly. No interest. This is a no-strings-attached gift. Please. It would mean a lot to me." I felt horrified at his reaction and his lack of trust in me.

Jake looked right at me. "Why?"

"I want to help, and . . . I want to be friends."

"Money can't buy you everything, you know," said Jake. "Especially friends."

"Yes, of course. You're right. I'm so sorry. Okay. Forget the money. Sorry. I didn't mean to be offensive. I really didn't, but . . . I genuinely would like you to be my friend. It would mean a lot to me."

Jake nodded slowly. "Okay. Seeing as it's Christmas, and even though you are a totally obnoxious witch, you are also pretty funny. I will be your friend."

Marilyn rolled her eyes. "Oh, for heaven's sake, Jake," she said, "take the cash, too. Your family needs it, and we can all see that she's being straight for once in her life."

"I am, but it's your choice, Jake," I said. "The money's still on the table if you want it."

The room fell silent as Jake considered the offer. After a few moments, he took a deep breath, coughed, and then nodded. "Okay, then. Deal."

"Deal," I said.

Mr. O. beamed happily around the room. "Okay. So who's next?"

"You can give me a pile of cash if you want to," said

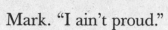

Mark. "I ain't proud."

I remembered his family in my dream last night. The worried expressions of his parents. "How about I give you something else instead of cash?"

"No. Money will be fine. And I'll be your friend too, if you like."

"How about instead of money, I buy your family a house?"

Mark sighed and looked sad. "Okay, so now I know that you're mesing around. A dollhouse, right? You're just joking, aren't you?"

I turned to Mr. O. "Tell him, tell him that I mean it."

Mr. O. nodded. "She's serious."

"I am," I said. "Look. I know that I've been a pain since I got here and acted like a brat princess, but . . . well, a few things have become clear to me—like what matters. Family is one thing. Having a home is another. And friends, too. So, Mark, I'd like to help, if you'll let me. As one friend to another. I'd like to buy your family a house. A real one. Okay, not a mansion, but a house. A home from where you can't be evicted." Mark's expression looked so hopeful that I knew I could never let him down. "I *really* mean it, don't I, Mr. O.? Tell him."

Mr. O. nodded. "She does. And she can. And I think she will."

Mark fell back onto his bed with a huge silly grin.

"Mom and Dad are going to be so . . . wow! This is *amazing*. Like winning the lottery. The best Christmas present ever."

Lynn sidled up to me. "What about me?" she asked, and then she sighed. "I don't need a house. Or medical help. What are you gonna give me, princess?"

I already knew what I'd like to give Lynn. I'd decided days ago. Long before the dreams and my encounters with Saturn, Neptune, and Pluto. I knew that I wanted to give her some type of present because of all of them, in her own weird way, she had befriended me the most. "Don't you remember what you wanted?" I asked.

She shook her head.

"But you *told* me what you want, Lynn. Friends. A pet. Pets are the best friends because they never judge you and never let you down. Remember, I told you about my dog, Coco? I suggest that we go next week and get whatever you want. A rabbit, a dog, a cat, a goldfish. Whatever you want."

Lynn sniffed and pulled an "I'm not impressed" face. "Yeah. Okay. Cool. Yeah. Maybe a rottweiler. Or a piranha—you know, those fish that eat flesh—or . . . a man-eating spider or a boa constrictor. What do you think?"

I must have looked shocked. I hadn't imagined that she'd want *killer* pets, but then she grinned. "Just messin' with you, Leo. No. A couple of cutie-pie kittens would be perfect."

"And what about Marilyn?" asked Mr. O.

"I don't want anything," pouted Marilyn. "I don't need anything from 'er."

"Oh, cut the tough act, Marilyn," I said. "I wouldn't leave you out, and . . . although we haven't been the best of friends, we have been through a lot in here together. Please let me give you something too."

"I don't know if I want to be friends. You can't buy me as easily as the others."

"I'm not trying to buy you! I am trying to be NICE for a change . . ." I could feel a major tantrum coming on. *or heaven's sake*, I thought, *I try to do the decent thing, and boy, are they making it hard work!* I turned to Mr. O. and looked at him pleadingly. "I am *trying* to be good here, and all I am getting back is *ingratitude* and *suspicion*!"

Mr. O. coughed. "Now then, Leonora, you haven't exactly been Princess Perfect since you got here. Can you blame them for being suspicious of your motives?"

I looked around at the group and had to admit that I hadn't exactly shown my *best* side. "Okay. Sorry. Sorry. You don't have to be my friend, Marilyn, not if you don't want to. Just, I thought that I could give you a shopping spree. The shopping spree that I was going to go on before I came here. In fact, I'll come with you if you want. It's always more fun if you go with a friend . . . not that you have to be my friend . . . no, I mean, it's more fun to go with someone. Oh, never mind. Look. I know all the best boutiques in Paris, and I don't really need any more clothes, so you can have my allowance as well. I have enough stuff. Well, okay, almost enough. Maybe I *could* use a couple of pairs of shoes and a handbag and a . . . actually . . . maybe I need a whole new wardrobe, since I am about a million times thinner now than when I came in here. Yeah, come to think of it, I need *loads* of things. Yeah. I should come with you."

Mr. O. and the boys cracked up laughing, and for a second I saw myself through their eyes.

"Oops! I'm doing the me-me-me thing again, aren't I? Sorry. Old habits blah-de-blah. Anyway. Shopping. You. Me. Beautiful Paris. Are you up for it, Marilyn?"

Marilyn shrugged. "Yeah, maybe," she said. "If you play your cards right and don't go back to being the brat princess. I'll come with you if you be yourself. The *real* Leonora. You don't have to pretend to be some sister of mercy all of a sudden. I don't buy it."

"Okay," I agreed.

"And can I say something to you, now that we're talking about fashion?" Marilyn continued.

I nodded.

"You look so much better with your hair curly. It suits your personality to be wild. It's like a manifestation of your character."

"Yeah. And your eyes look better brown," added Lynn. "Better with your coloring."

"Yeah," chorused Jake and Mark.

"Huh," I said, and I rolled my eyes up to the ceiling. "Like I'm going to listen to a bunch of losers like you for fashion advice."

For a moment their faces dropped.

"Only joking," I said. Actually, I was pleased with my new look. I could see for myself that I looked a lot better. I was in better shape, too. The zits were gone. And it was a relief not to have to spend hours straightening my hair every morning.

"You know what, princess?" said Lynn. "You're all right. You're going to fit in after all. Isn't she, Marilyn?"

Marilyn nodded. "Yeah. And . . . well . . . we have something to say to you, too. We were pulling your leg, weren't we? About being murderers and all."

I creased up laughing. "I knew that. You're not tough enough!"

"You neither," Marilyn said, smiling. "You know, I guess we're not that different after all. We both put on an act. And we both have parents who are under some crazy presumption that being here might make us nicer people."

"As if," said Lynn.

"Yeah," said Marilyn. She looked awkward for a moment. "I was teased about my background at my last school—that's why I put on the tough accent here, so that no one would make fun of me."

"No need," I said. "We won't bully you here."

"No way," said Mark.

"Now what about you, Leonora?" asked Mr. O. "Is there anything that you want?"

"Um . . . could I possibly have my credit cards back?"

Mr. O. nodded. "I think that can be arranged, but I think I know what you have in mind, and you might not need them, as Jupiter is . . ."

"You going to organize a private plane out of here?" Jake interrupted.

I shook my head. "No. Not just yet, because . . . if I'm allowed, I'd like to help make Christmas special. Right here. If you'll let me . . ." I glanced over at Mr. O., and he nodded. "Okay, we're going to have the best Christmas breakfast and lunch ever. And roaring fires. And games. And presents. And chocolates. And . . ."

Lynn shrieked. "And *snow!*"

I nodded. "Well, that would be nice, but I'm not sure that you can get snow with American Express . . ."

Lynn pointed up at the window. She was right. It had started to snow. I raced to the window and saw that the sky was heavy with black clouds, and white flakes had begun to fall, coating the lawn and the trees and shrubs outside. It looked so magical as the rising sun caught the flakes and made them sparkle with a million tiny stars.

"And hey," cried Jake, "Joe's back!"

"As I was trying to tell you, you won't have to wait long for that Christmas breakfast," said Mr. O.

There outside the kitchen door was the man from the deli. Joe. He was dressed up as Santa, and he was unloading the best breakfast feast that I had ever seen. He saw us watching him, gave us a cheery wave, and beckoned us to go to the kitchen.

The others made a dash for it, but I held back for a few moments.

"Not joining the others?" asked Mr. O.

"In a sec," I said. "I just wanted to say thank you, whoever you are, a planet, a guardian, or whatever. You've been great, and, even in this dismal place, it's clear that you're a real star."

Mr. O. flushed pink with pleasure. "You, too, Leonora. You too." Then he cleared his throat and offered me his arm. "Now, let's go eat and get warm. And it's about time, I say, because, you think this place has been an ordeal for you? Ha! I can tell you now—dingy, cold places are *not* my scene at all. So let's go light a few fires, get that feast organized, and have ourselves a very merry Christmas."

"Sounds like a great plan," I said with a grin as I took his arm.

Epilogue

I got to go home on New Year's Day. Mommy and Daddy were in the hall at the lodge just after breakfast and had a helicopter waiting in the grounds outside to whisk me away. It was wonderful to see their kind, familiar faces again.

Before we returned to the Caribbean, I went to a store and bought an angel's outfit, complete with white feather wings and a halo (not for me—I wasn't that deluded!). I gave it to Shirla when I got home to give to her granddaughter so that she could be a Christmas angel after all. It was my way of saying sorry for being such an almighty pain for so long, and I think that Shirla was really touched.

My new pal Mr. O. came to visit us in the Caribbean. He said that he likes the climate better there, and, while he was with us, he confessed that I was one of his favorite Zodiac Girls because I was his biggest challenge. I never did get whether the zodiac thing was legit or whether he was actually certifiable and, with the rest of his strange friends, a candidate for la-la land. He never mentioned it again after my month as a Zodiac Girl, and neither did I. Whatever. In the end, it didn't matter. We got a result, and that's what counts. One of the unexpected bonuses from my time at the boot camp was that I looked a whole lot better. Everyone commented. No zits or flab. And I've stayed as slim as I was in the lodge. Okay, so I'm not a size zero, but I don't want to be anymore. I want to feel good and be healthy. I came out of the boot camp feeling great and put it down to the simple fresh food we had in there and plenty of exercise. Shirla, Coco, and I go jogging along the beach most days now, and Mason's learned to cook delicious meals that aren't fattening. He can even make oatmeal taste divine with fresh fruit. (There was no way I was going to keep eating it the way that they served it at the lodge. I don't believe in suffering beyond the call of duty.)

I stayed in touch with my boot-camp inmates, and they are among my closest friends, although we live in different countries. (Mommy and Daddy got me into a local school, so I don't have to board and be away from them anymore.) All of them e-mail regularly, and we speak on the phone when we can. Marilyn and Lynn went back to their school and were elected to run the school bookstore, with great successs. Mark decided that he wanted to be an actor, specializing in mime. I think that he'll be good at it, and, from his e-mails, it sounds like he is happy now that he knows what he wants to do with his life and has a secure home. Sadly, although Jake's brother went on to make a terrific recovery, Jake never did get over his addiction to joyriding. After stealing a silver Mercedes, he got caught driving the wrong way down a highway singing "God Save the Queen" with his pants on his head at 4:00 A.M. Luckily, he didn't hit anyone or anything, but he was locked up for two years. *C'est la vie.* You can't win them all.

And in case you're wondering if I let Shirla, Mason, or Henry out of their debts—no way! Excuse me, do I look like sucker of the year? But I *did* let them out of the interest. I'm not a total Scrooge. They earn a ton of money compared to other people, so give me a break, I'm not the *only* person who had lessons to learn. Like, reality check—they shouldn't have been borrowing money from a 14-year-old head case who didn't know any better!

The best news, though, was that, the year after my time in the boot camp, I was on the front cover of *Teen Vogue*, and there was an article about me inside, saying, "I was the teenager who knew best how to keep Christmas alive and happy." A fact I pride myself on, actually. Oh, yes. I am the queen of generosity, I really am. Oh, yes. Bring it on and deck the halls with boughs of holly, yada yada yada. I'll be there. Every year in December. Okay, so maybe on a yacht somewhere fabulous. But, why not? I can afford it, and hey—'tis the season to be jolly.

So, really. Peace on Earth and God bless us. Every one.

The Leo Files

Characteristics, Facts, and Fun

July 24–August 23

Loyal and proud, Leos are vibrant and larger than life. Leos love to be noticed and admired, and they will do anything to gain your attention. This sign is creative, and they will push themselves until they reach the top of whatever ladder they happen to be climbing!

Although there's always something interesting going on around a Leo, don't forget to duck when they don't get their own way. These guys can be arrogant, proud, pushy, and haughty. They like to receive compliments, so if you haven't given them one for a while, expect to get some of the famous fiery Leo temper!

Element:	Fire
Color:	Gold, orange
Birthstone:	Ruby, diamond
Animal:	Dog
Lucky day:	Sunday
Planet:	Ruled by the Sun

Leo's best friends are likely to be:
Aries
Sagittarius
Libra

Leo's enemies are likely to be:
Virgo
Scorpio

A Leo's idea of heaven would be:
If it was their birthday every day—constant attention and compliments!

A Leo would go crazy if:
They were required to clean, cook, and wait on other people.

Famous Leos:
Madonna
Arnold Schwarzenegger
J. K. Rowling
Bill Clinton
Robert De Niro
Halle Berry

Here's the first chapter of another fantastic
Zodiac Girls story, **Discount Diva**.

Chapter One

The Crazy Maisies

I wish, I wish, I wish I could go, I thought when our teacher Miss Creighton first made the announcement.

". . . I will be taking names from all you eighth-grade girls in the next week," she continued. "All those who want to go must register before the end of May, which only gives you two weeks."

A school trip to Venice. Two weeks in sunny Italy. I wanted to go more than anything, ever, since the beginning of eternity and even before that.

"You going to put your name down, Tori?" asked Georgie when the bell rang and we headed out of the classroom for our lunch break.

I shrugged my shoulders as if I didn't really care. "Maybe," I said.

"I definitely am," said Megan, catching up with us and linking arms. "Mom said I could go on the next school trip, wherever it was."

"Me, too," said Hannah, linking arms with Megan.

"Me, too," said Georgie. "Which means *you have* to come, Tori. It wouldn't be the same without you. The Crazy Maisies hit Europe."

Me, Hannah, Megan, and Georgie. We called ourselves the Crazy Maisies. My mom used to call me that when I was little and acting silly. Me and my friends act silly a lot, hence the name.

"Venice isn't *that* great," I said. "Too many tourists. Florence is much more interesting." Ha. Like I'd been to either of them. Not. But I had heard my well-traveled Aunt Phoebe saying that Venice was so full of tourists these days that you could hardly move.

"You *have* to come," said Hannah. "And so what if there are loads of tourists? We'll be four of them!"

"Yeah," said Georgie. "Italy, here we come!"

I felt a sinking feeling in my stomach. I was *so* going to miss out, but I could never tell them the real reason why I couldn't go.

"Si, signora, pasta, cappuccino, tiramisu," I said, trying to remember all the Italianish words that I had ever heard and to distract them from trying to persuade me to go. I'd have to think up some excuse that they'd all buy later.

"Linguine, Botticelli, spaghetti . . ." Megan joined in.

"Da Vinci, Madonna, pizzeria, Roma," said Hannah.

Then they started singing a song that we'd done in music class last quarter. We'd had a substitute teacher who had us singing songs from around the globe. "Trying to broaden your horizons," he said as he taught us folk songs from Italy to Iceland. By the end of the quarter, however, I think he was glad to broaden his horizons and move on to another school where the students weren't tone-deaf.

"When the moon hits your eye like a big pizza pie, that's *amore* . . ." my friends chorused off-key and in terrible Italian accents.

A few ninth-grade girls sloped past and looked at us as if we were crazy. I play-acted that I wasn't with them, but Georgie dragged me back, and Hannah and Megan got down on their knees, put their hands on their hearts, and continued hollering away at the tops of their voices.

Crazy. They all are. And they'll have a great time in Venice, that's for sure. Another thing that was for sure was that no way would I be going with them. Not a hope in heck.

During break, we went out into the playground, found a bench on the sunny side, and did each other's hair. When we first met, only Georgie, out of the four of us, had long hair. After a short time hanging out together, we all decided to grow our hair to the same length so that we could play hairdresser, and long hair is best for experimenting with. Georgie and Meg are blond, although Megan's hair is thicker and golden blond, while

Georgie's is fine white-blond. Hannah and I have ordinary brown hair, although Hannah has had chestnut highlights put in hers lately. It looks totally cool. I'd love to have highlights, but that's another thing to add to the "not going to happen unless Mom wins the lottery" list.

I think Georgie's the prettiest of the four of us, although Megan and Hannah are good-looking in their own ways too. Hannah could pass for being Mexican. She has olive skin and amazing dark brown eyes, which look enormous when she puts on makeup, and Megan has a sweet face, cornflower-blue eyes, and a tiny nose like a doll. Out of all of us, boys mostly pay attention to Georgie and me, though. Hannah and Megan say it's because I'm pretty too, but sometimes I wonder if the main reason that boys talk to me is to get in with Georgie.

I'm not huge in the confidence department. Some days I can look okay—I know I can—but I could look lots better if I got my hair done professionally and bought some fab new clothes and makeup, but I doubt if that's going to happen anytime soon. Reason being, my family is broke and a half, so it's hard trying to keep up on the appearance front. Most of my clothes come from secondhand stores, but I worry that my friends will find out. At school, girls who don't wear the latest designer clothes get called Discount Divas because their clothes don't have recognizable labels. Megan, Georgie, and Hannah have no idea that I'm Queen Discount Diva.

"I think we should go for a really sophisticated look when we're in Venice," said Megan as she pulled back Georgie's hair and began to braid it.

"No. I think we should wear it loose," said Hannah.

"Yeah," said Georgie. "Loose and romantic-looking. There might be some cute Italian boys to flirt with."

Oh, no! Boys! Italian boys. I hadn't thought of that. What if one of my friends got a boyfriend and I wasn't there to share it all with them? What if all *three* of them got boyfriends and had their first kiss? It might happen. I've heard that Italy is a really romantic place. *Romeo and Juliet* happened over there, and they were *way* loved up. I've also heard that Italian boys are very hot-blooded. (I'm not totally sure what that means and whether they really do have hotter blood than us on account of living in a warmer climate. Whatever.) Apparently they are more forward than American boys, who mostly seem more interested in computers than they do in girls. Anyway, I would be left so far behind in the game of love. I'd be like Cinderella left at home while everyone else went to the ball. Eek! That would be freaking *tragic.* The Crazy Maisies do everything new together—that way we can talk about it all and see how we all feel.

"Ow," said Hannah with a wince as I brushed her hair up into a ponytail. "You're hurting me."

"Sorry," I said and made myself brush more gently. I didn't mean to take my frustration out on her, but all the talk for the next few weeks would be about the trip. And then they'd go, and I'd be by myself. And then they'd come back, and all the talk would be about the trip again. And I'd have nothing to say because I wouldn't have been there. I'd be left out. It would be awful.

Luckily, Megan changed the subject and began making plans for the weekend. A new comedy was playing at the local movie theater. Of course, everyone was up for seeing it.

"Cool!" said Georgie. "And we could go for a snack afterward."

Megan and Hannah nodded enthusiastically. "Lots of those spicy, cheesy taco thingies. I loooove them."

"Ice cream for me," said Georgie. "Pistachio with . . . strawberry."

"Pecan fudge is my fave," I joined in.

"We'll have to do the early show, around six o'clock, or Mom won't be able to pick me up," said Hannah.

I did a quick calculation as they were discussing how they were going to get there and back and what they were going to eat. I'd need money for the movie. Snack. Coke. Nope. No way could I do it on my allowance money. I get around one fourth of what my friends get, and some weeks when things are really tight, Mom can't give us anything at all—us being me, my older sister, Andrea, and my two brothers, William and Daniel. I took a deep breath and got ready to apply my usual philosophy: when the going gets tough, the tough bluff it.

"I can't make it tonight. Mom got me and Dan and Will tickets for the Cyber Queens gig."

"The Cyber Queens? Wow! You *lucky* thing!" said Georgie.

"You've kept quiet about that this week," said Megan. "Those tickets are like the hottest in town."

Hannah playfully punched my arm. "Yeah. Why didn't you tell us?"

"Mom only told us last night. It was a surprise for when we got home."

"A surprise? That's *so* cool," said Georgie. "Your mom is so awesome. I wish my mom did stuff like that. I bet my mom hasn't even *heard* of the Cyber Queens. Can she get the rest of us tickets?"

"Don't think so," I replied. "I think she got the last ones."

"Take your digital camera," said Hannah. "Take lots of pictures to show us."

"Sure," I said.

I felt guilty when the bell rang for afternoon classes. Not only did I not have tickets for the Cyber Queens, but I don't have a digital camera either, even though I'd told everyone that my grandma had gotten me one as an early birthday present. I lied. I don't really like doing it, but sometimes it's necessary. I have to make things up so that they don't think that I'm a total loser. My friends have rich parents who buy them all the latest stuff: iPods, cell phones with cameras, computer games, designer clothes. They've all got their own TVs *and* their own computers in their bedrooms. I don't even have my own bedroom. Not even my own bed. Not really. I have to share a room and a bunk bed with my sister, Andrea. Sometimes I sleep on the downstairs sofa just to get a bit of space, although even then I have to share it—with our cats, Midnight and Meatloaf. (My brother Will named them. Midnight's black, and Meatloaf is a dark tabby.)

Anyway, my friends would surely dump me if they knew the truth about my situation and how poor we really are compared to them. When we first all started hanging out together as a group at the beginning of this year, to dissuade them from coming over, I told them that our house was being redecorated from top to bottom—kitchen, bathroom, the whole thing. I keep telling the girls that we're having "nightmares" with the workers, who keep letting us down. It's an expression that I've heard their parents use a million times.

So far, they haven't been over a lot, but when they have been, my excuses have worked, because the fact is, our house does look like it's in the middle of being redecorated. The walls are patchy with daubs of paint here and there where we decided to try out some paint samples but there wasn't enough cash to buy the paint. There are no carpets on the stairs. The carpets that are down on the floor are worn. There are floorboards up here and there. The whole place looks like it needs to be ripped out and redone from top to toe, so my story has never met with any questions.

Sometimes I think that Georgie may have caught on, but she's never come out and said anything, not yet anyway. It can be stressful on the rare occasions when the girls do come over since I'm afraid that Andrea, Will, or Dan might blow my cover. Instead, I try and make sure that we hang out at Megan, Hannah, or Georgie's houses. I tell them that the floor's up again or the water's off or something. They're so sympathetic that I feel rotten, especially since Georgie seems to like coming to our house, and she always brings something with her, like some fab muffins or expensive chocolate cookies or elderflower juice (my fave).

All my friends are kind. They invite me to sleep over at their houses when I lay on the construction nightmare scenario really thick—like last week I said that a plumber had caused a burst pipe and there was water everywhere. I like going to Georgie's place the best. It's awesome. They have five bedrooms at her house for just her and her mom. *Five*. And seeing as Georgie is an only child, that means that they have three spare. *Three*. I wish I could go and live with her sometimes, although I know deep down that I'd miss my family and especially the cats. Her house is like a palace compared to where I live; I feel like a princess when I'm there, and her mom never interferes with her life. Not like my house. No privacy there. Not even in the bathroom, as there is always someone knocking on the door telling whoever is in there to hurry up.

Some days, like today, being poor stinks. It is Friday. May 12th. The whole world would be out enjoying the early summer sun this evening. Certainly half of our school would be. Everyone down at the local theater to watch a movie and hang out. Some of the older girls from our school would also be there, showing off the fab new outfits they'd just got. There would probably even be some boys there from Marborough High down the road. And I'd have to miss out on the whole outing because I haven't got enough money to go.

As we got up to go back into school, there was a sudden blast of wind, blowing up dust and debris from the playground.

"Whoa," said Georgie as her skirt billowed up. "Where's that come from?"

"Dunno," said Meg, "but let's run."

In an instant, more papers and candy wrappers began to blow in a mini tornado around the playground as the kids headed back inside. A piece of paper flew toward me and stuck to my hand. I flicked it off, but it fluttered back again, and we all laughed, because after I brushed it off for the second time, it seemed to follow me as we headed back to the classroom. It was dancing along behind me, and just before I reached the door, it blew right up until it covered my face so that I couldn't see.

"Bleurgh," I blustered as I pulled it away from my eyes.

"Maybe it's meant for you," said Megan, taking the paper away from me. "Let's see what it is."

"Yeah, right," I said. "Maybe it's a message from a fairy." I was teasing her because last year she was into fairies and angels, and her bedroom was covered with posters of them.

"What does it say?" asked Hannah.

Megan scanned the paper. "Dear Tori, You are to go to the bluebell dell at midnight on Friday night . . ."

I punched her arm playfully. I knew she was making that up. "What does it really say?"

"It looks like some sort of promotion-type thing," she replied. "Um . . . advertising local businesses kind of thing. A beauty salon in Osbury. A café/deli. An astrology website. Stuff like that."

"I'll chuck it," I said and took it to put it in the garbage can in the corner of the playground. As I threw it away, there was a flash of lightning and then a rumble of thunder in the distance. I glanced up. The sky had darkened, threatening sudden rain, so I raced back to join the others at the door.

"The fairies are angry that you threw away their business promotion," joked Georgie.

"Yeah, right. Fairies and elves are alive and well and

have taken over Osbury." I laughed back.

Seconds later, the sky opened, and rain pelted down, so we darted inside as quick as we could.

"Phew," I said as we raced along the corridors. "Just made it."

As we settled into class, our teacher, Miss Wilkins, was busy closing the windows that had been open earlier in the morning. The rain continued pouring down, and the wind was still whipping up debris outside. As she reached the last window at the back of the class near my desk, a piece of paper blew in. It sailed right across the classroom and landed *plonk* in front of me.

Meg, Hannah, and Georgie turned to look. I glanced down. It was the same piece of paper that had been following me in the playground! Beauty salon, deli, astrology website . . .

Maybe Megan was right and there were fairies and guardian angels out there. Maybe this was a message from one of them in code or something. *Yeah. And I'm the richest girl in the world*, I thought. However, the paper arriving in front of me did make me wonder. I didn't believe in fairyland like Meg did, but I *did* believe that some things are meant to be. Like fate. Or destiny. And *this* was a coincidence. I couldn't deny that. Maybe it *was* meant for me. I was about to put the paper in my backpack to look at it more carefully later when Miss Wilkins closed the last window and turned back to the class. As she did, she saw the paper that had landed on my desk.

"That garbage is blowing everywhere!" she said as she picked it up, ripped it into tiny pieces, and took it to the front of the room, where she threw it away. "Such a nuisance."

Oh, no, I thought as I watched her do it. *There goes the message about my destiny—straight into the trash!*